Just Stay

More Than Friends #4

Aria Grace

Just Stay

Published by Surrendered Press

Copyright 2014 Aria Grace

CHAPTER ONE

SPENCER

Sometimes reality is crazier than even the most ridiculous dramatic thriller. Four days ago, my biggest worries were which keynote speaker invitation I should accept for next year's conference circuit and whether to pull the trigger on a cabin in Lake Tahoe or Vail.

And now I'm sitting in an ambulance with a guy I've known for less than twenty-four hours but that took a bullet for me a few minutes ago. How did this all happen? Oh yeah, my good buddy Steve asked for a favor.

Seemed simple enough. Show up in Portland and pretend to be interested in buying rare art from some asshole that was forging it without sharing the proceeds with his Mafioso family. It sounded like an adventure with minimal risk. It was also my way of helping out Steve. He's a good guy that has been afraid to let down his guard after a painful breakup a few years back.

I'd like to think it was my sense of loyalty that made me so eager to agree but really it was as much out of boredom as it was out of sentimentality. My life of board meetings and investor calls and product reviews has added many zeros to my bank balance but is completely unfulfilling in almost every other way.

The gossip rags have labeled me as one of Silicon Valley's most eligible bachelors but I can't remember the last time I had a date. The men I meet are either intimidated by my wealth, only interested in getting a piece of it, or just aren't interesting to me. I don't want to date a mirror image of myself. Where is the intrigue in that? I might as well just stroke off to a mirror.

I also can't remember the last time I met someone I was attracted to *and* interested in that wasn't falling over himself to get in my wallet.

Dylan had no idea who I was other than a rich guy interested in some art. I wouldn't even have realized he was interested if I didn't catch him staring the whole time we talked about the art I was looking to acquire. When Matty, my fake realtor, introduced me to Dylan, assistant and bodyguard to the asshole forger I was there to take down, I was immediately smitten.

I don't normally look for really buff guys because they aren't usually interested in skinny computer nerds like myself. But I couldn't keep my eyes off him while Matty went through the motions of discussing the apartment I was there to look at and the type of art that was needed to fill it.

Dylan's light blue eyes were almost grey when the cloudy afternoon reflected in from the penthouse windows. The way they kept moving to my mouth whether I was speaking or not had my stomach in knots.

I wouldn't have believed someone with his wide build would seem almost shy around me. I'm basically the king of dorks, complete with Coke bottle glasses and the same haircut I've had since I was six.

But he gave me the signals I'm not normally tuned into. I'd just decided to bite the bullet and ask him out when our little charade fell into complete chaos.

I'd handed over the cash for the paintings and was on my way out of the apartment, exactly as we'd planned it, when Topher DeMonaco figured us out. He found the gun Matty was wearing and turned it on me.

My adventure was coming to an end. As I looked down the barrel of that gun, I wondered briefly if Dylan would have said yes when I asked him out. My question was answered when he stepped in front of me, shielding my heart with his thickly muscled shoulder and taking the bullet that was supposed to be mine.

The full weight of his powerful body jerked into my arms. In shock, and not sure if I'd also been hit, my knees buckled and we both landed on the ground. Dylan was conscious but confused about why his boss wanted to shoot me.

"Shhh, it's okay," I said, admiring the chiseled lines of his jaw. The light dusting of stubble across his cheeks called out to me. Trying to convince myself it was purely to keep him calm and conscious, I rested my cheek against his and spoke into his ear. "You're gonna be okay. Just try not to move."

He nodded against me, scratching a line of tingles into my smooth skin.

"I'm so sorry you got dragged into this."

"Into what?" He pulled away and looked me in the eyes. "What's going on? Who are you?"

I didn't want to see hurt or deception in his eyes but it was there, blending in with the confusion he felt. "I'm who I said I was. I promise." I pressed my hand over the nick in his shoulder that was spewing more blood than I'd ever been in contact with. "We just didn't expect this Topher guy to bring his muscle with him."

"You were trying to get to Topher?" he asked, straining his neck to see what was happening behind him.

"Hey, focus on me. Don't worry about them right now." In my periphery, I could see Topher holding the gun up to Matty but I didn't break eye contact with Dylan. "I was asked to help out a friend. I didn't know I'd end up with the hulk in my lap before dinner and drinks."

Dylan still had enough blood in his system to color his tanned skin a beautiful plum shade. "I don't know about that."

"I do." I was about to press my lips to his forehead when a group of large bikers filled the entryway.

"Uncle Sal?" Topher looked around the room, confused about what was happening. "What are you doing here?"

A huge skin head stepped forward and reached for Topher's gun. Dylan stilled in my lap at the name. He knew what Uncle Sal's presence meant for his boss.

"You're okay." I whispered to him. "I promise."

He held my gaze, pulling me into the clear blue pools that had my attention since the moment I met him. He nodded and shifted his weight slightly so he was between my legs. I wanted to scoot him away from whatever was about to go down but I didn't dare move. It was one of those situations where playing possum is your best bet at survival.

As quickly as they came in, the gang of bikers walked out of the apartment with a whining Topher wedged in their circle. Once the elevator doors closed, Dylan dropped his forehead to my chest and let out a deep sigh.

His breath was almost steady when he noticed the cute blond inching toward him with a guilty expression on his face.

"Oh, god, Dylan. I'm so sorry." The boy was in tears as he approached us.

"Joey?" Dylan shook his head like he was looking at a ghost. "Is that you?"

Joey stepped forward and reached for Dylan's good hand. "It's me." He choked out another sob. "And he's gone, Dylan. Topher is gone."

Dylan looked at me then around then room. "I don't understand. What are you talking about?"

Joey was cut off when paramedics entered the room and took Dylan out of my arms. His eyes didn't leave mine as they began to assess his injury and measure his vitals.

CHAPTER TWO

DYLAN

The last twenty minutes of my life are a jumbled mess. I can picture every scene in my head but they don't make much sense when put together. And how I ended up in the back of an ambulance with some undercover art buyer is still a bit hazy.

All I know for sure is I'm on my left side and staring into the turquoise eyes that haven't left my line of sight since the paramedics showed up. Spencer is partially the reason I've got a bullet hole in my right shoulder but I'd do it again.

He's from California and by the way he carries himself, he's probably some genius computer engineer that has never shot at anything more angry than a cartoon bird on his phone.

He's clearly not from this world. I grew up playing with Topher DeMonaco and was eager to take the job he offered after I finished college. I thought being the assistant to an entertainment mogul would be a great experience. I want to open a club myself and figured it'd be a great way to learn the business. I just didn't know that Topher's *business* included indentured prostitutes and drug trafficking for the Mexican mafia.

The words Joey said come to the front of my mind. I look down at Spencer's mouth before licking my lips and asking, "What did Joey mean?"

"About what?" Spencer leans forward with his elbows on his knees. His face is close enough that

I can feel his warm breath on my cheek, almost tickling my ear.

"When he said Topher is gone." If my right arm didn't feel detached from my body, I would have reached out to straighten Spencer's hair. His previously neat auburn hair is now sticking up in every direction. As I'm looking at the wayward strands, he runs his hand through it again, making the few flat sections stand up at various angles. *Damn, he's adorable.*

"His uncle is dealing with him." Spencer presses closer to my ear, the heat of his face warming mine. "But you'll probably need to find another job."

My eyes close as his words sink in. Topher is gone. I'm no longer indebted to him. When he paid off over $100k in student loans, I thought it was something like a hiring bonus but it was more of a deed to my life. Topher expected me to spend the next ten years working as his bodyguard with only simple business related duties. By the time I figured it out, there was no way to leave.

That was three years ago and now I might be free. Free to begin my life without Topher controlling every move I make. I have no idea where to start. My mind is flitting through options when the back doors to the van open up and I'm pulled out into the windy evening.

"Sir, you're at County Med. They're gonna take care of you, okay?"

I nod and turn my head into the pad I'm lying on. My eye lids close to shield them from the bright overhead lights as I'm wheeled down a long corridor. I'm answering questions that seem to be coming from a distant voice but I'm not paying attention to who's asking or what they mean.

The adrenaline that was fueling me is wearing off and the pain is unbearable. I just want to sleep. I'm almost out when I feel cold air on my hand.

My eyes shoot open in time to see Spencer watching me just before a pair of swinging doors close around him, blocking him from my view.

~**~

Blessed sleep comes but not enough of it. I'm jostled awake by a nurse wrapping gauze under my armpit. I can see her movements but I don't feel any pain. Maybe it was a dream. Maybe a nightmare. No, not a nightmare.

Those bright blue eyes were too stunning to come from a nightmare. Even through the thick glass, they pulled me in and I couldn't look away. Definitely a dream. Or a fantasy.

"Hey, you're awake." I squeeze my eyes shut then open them again to make sure I'm fully awake.

"Hmm." I turn slightly and see Spencer standing at the foot of the bed. "You're here?"

His face blanches and he looks uncomfortable. "Uh, yeah. Sorry. I just didn't know who to call and didn't want to leave you alone."

"No." I have to clear my throat a few times before I can speak through the cottony feeling. "I didn't mean it like that."

I look toward the nurse. "Can I get some water?"

She glances at me for just a second before turning back to her ball of gauze. "I'll get it for you in just a second."

"I got it." Spencer is already holding a blue cup with a bendy straw up to my mouth.

I try to take it from his hands but I'm a little shaky and spill a few drops on the sheet covering me. "Shit."

"Here." He positions the straw at my lips. "Just take a drink while I hold it."

I feel stupid as I take the straw in my mouth and inhale but the cool water feels so good going down that I get over it pretty quick. Draining the cup, I hold the last drops in my mouth for a moment, saturating the dry tissue. "Thanks."

"Yeah." He awkwardly puts the cup on a rolling tray then pats my hand. "So, is there anyone I should call? Someone waiting at home that can pick you up?"

The memory of his less than subtle admission about being single makes me smile just a bit. I wonder if he's trying to get more info or if he's genuinely wondering who to call. Either way, I know he's busy and probably needs to get out of here.

"No." I laugh. "Actually, I usually stay at Topher's place so I'm kinda homeless."

"Seriously." Spencer and the nurse both look at me with concern.

"Well, yeah, but it's fine." I wince as the nurse lowers my arm. "I'll call my sister and see if I can stay with her."

"I can call her if you give me her number." Spencer pulls out his phone to dial but the glare from the nurse stops him. "Well, I'll take her number and go outside to call."

He's obviously a rule follower. Definitely not from my world.

"Uh, what time is it?" I don't see my phone but Spencer quickly pulls out his.

"It's eleven forty." He slips his phone back in his jacket pocket and glances out the window. "Is it too late to call her?"

"Probably. I wouldn't want to wake the baby." I glance at the nurse. "Uh, actually, I'm good for tonight. I can just take a cab."

The nurse cocks an eyebrow. "Are you sure?"

"Of course." I smile despite the throbbing pressure that's coming back with a vengeance. "As long as you give me something for the pain, I'll be fine."

"I'll make sure he has a warm bed tonight." Spencer speaks up with more authority than I've seen from him.

Will you now? I glance at him and can't help the smirk that pulls my lip out to one side. "Right. I'll be in good hands."

Spencer goes red as he steps closer to my chest and looks to the nurse. "So, is he allowed to leave?"

"The doctor and detective have both cleared him to leave when he's ready." She looks me over from head to toe. "Since it was just a nick, you'll probably be fine with over the counter stuff but I'm sending you home with a script for Motrin in case you need something stronger."

I nod and tug at the hospital gown that's creatively tied around my neck and snapped around my left side. "I guess my shirt is a lost cause?"

Spencer laughs as the nurse hangs a clipboard on the end of the bed and quietly walks out.

"Yeah…they put it in a bag but I don't think you're gonna want to wear it." He tugs on the lapel of his jacket. "I'd give you this but I don't think you could fit one of your biceps through it."

Apparently, he's been checking me out. "It's cool." I start to unsnap the side of my gown. "I could use the fresh air."

Spencer's eyes are as big as saucers as I get the left side free from my body. I can't quite untie the lace around my neck with one hand. "Uh, can you get this…"

He takes a step closer then tentatively reaches for the tie. I'm holding one side as his hand closes around mine and pulls the string. His knuckles brush my jawline and I almost lean into it. It's so soft and smooth. Once the loose knot is free, the gown pools in my lap.

Spencer's eyes are immediately drawn to my chest. Topher and I spent a week in Miami last month and my deep tan hasn't faded much. I can feel his heavy gaze on my taut skin as he inspects every protruding muscle.

I haven't felt so admired in a long time. It feels good.

~**~

An aide wheels me to the ER exit and I stand on wobbly legs. Spencer is immediately at my side, guiding me toward a cab. He's only a few inches taller but I'm hunched forward a bit so my head lands comfortably at his shoulder. His palm is firmly seated against my back, warming me despite the coastal breeze settling in.

The irony of our situation is not lost on me. I'm the body building personal guard that hasn't physically leaned on anyone since I was twelve years old. Relying on this slim man that plotted to take down my boss and could have gotten me killed shouldn't even be within the realm of possibilities. But as much as I probably shouldn't, I do trust Spencer. His hold is solid and I can feel the ripples of his back muscles as I balance against him.

If I wasn't in pain and essentially homeless, I'd probably go for it. Have a night of fun before figuring out what to do with the rest of my life. On the several occasions I've caught him staring, it was as curious as it was concerned. And when my shirt came off, he couldn't adjust his jacket fast enough to hide the bulge in his pants.

"You first," Spencer says as he opens the door to a waiting cab.

"Thanks." I pull out of his grasp and lower myself onto the car seat. As the minutes tick by, the pain comes back exponentially. "Do you have my phone? I need to call someone to see where I can crash tonight."

Spencer opens the plastic bag the nurse handed him and digs out my phone. "Here you go. But you can stay with me tonight." His eyes drop to my chest then he turns toward the window. "I mean, I have a suite downtown that you can stay in. I'll be leaving early in the morning but you can use it as long as you want."

The confidence he had with the nurse just an hour ago is completely gone. He's back to that shy boy that can't look me in the eye. I know it's a bad idea and all I want to do is pass out but his offer is tempting. Showing up at a friend's house after midnight with a gunshot wound will be nothing but drama so I relent. "Yeah, okay. If you don't mind."

"I uh… I don't mind." He glances at me quickly with a small smile.

"Cool." I lean onto my left shoulder and close my eyes.

CHAPTER THREE

SPENCER

I knew he was built by the way his shirt pulled against his chest but I had no idea he was a sculpted masterpiece of manly perfection. Dylan's skin is beautifully tanned a deep bronze like he just stepped off a tropical beach. I can only imagine what he looks like below the tan line.

Or maybe he doesn't have a tan line? Shit, I'm getting hard just thinking about it. I avert my gaze to the dark streets of Portland. "The Westin on Alder, please."

"Sure thing." The driver waits for Dylan to get settled before pulling off the curb.

"Are you cold?" Dylan is curled up with his good shoulder against the seat back as I take off my jacket and lay it over him.

"Not really." He opens his eyes just a sliver then smiles. "But thanks."

"No problem." I clear my throat to get rid of the high pitched crack I keep hearing. "I'm just so sorry you were caught up in all this."

"Mmm. 'S okay." His whispered words are barely audible as he relents to the most recent dose of meds.

No. It's not. Dylan could have been killed because we fucked up the charade. I was almost out the door when Topher figured us out.

I flick a tear off my cheek as I look down at the sweet face of the man who took a bullet for me.

The man who is now homeless and jobless because I had to feed my hero complex and try to save the day for Steve and his boyfriend. Shit, I completely forgot about Steve.

I send a quick text to Matty.

Everything okay with Steve?

He responds back just as we're pulling into the hotel parking lot.

He's on his way home now. They're good. Dylan?

D is staying at my hotel tonight. I'm heading home in the morning. Call if you need anything.

Thanks, man. And have fun playing doctor with the bodyguard.

Yeah, I wish. I hop out my side of the car and run to the curbside to help Dylan out. He groggily accepts my hand and lets me pull him into my arms. While I fish out a few bills from my wallet, Dylan's nose is blowing warm air into my throat.

The heat goes straight to my dick as I slide my palm across his back and around his waist then carefully walk him to my room.

By the time we get into the suite, Dylan is fully alert and walking on his own. "Nice room, man."

"Thanks." I lead him into the bedroom where a king size bed is prominently displayed. "You can sleep in here. I have to leave early so I'll crash on the sofa bed so I don't wake you up."

"You're leaving?" The disappointment in his voice is a surprise to both of us. "I mean, I don't want to kick you out of your bed if you have to get up early. I can take the couch."

I shrug as I pull the heavy drapes closed. "It's fine. You need to rest. And, uh, if you want to stay here for a while, I can extend my reservation."

Dylan smiles then takes another look around the room. "Thanks but I don't think I can afford these digs. I'm more of a Best Western kinda guy."

"Yeah, me too. But it's on my account so feel free to stay for a while." I toss the bag of soiled clothes on the dresser then open the closet door. There are two thick robes hanging inside. "Here's a robe so you can get cleaned up. I might have a t-shirt or something that'll fit you."

Dylan looks down at his bare chest and picks a flake of blood off his abs. "Yeah, I guess I can't exactly go around like this all day."

"I doubt anyone would complain." Shit, did I say that out loud?

With a smirk, Dylan sits on the bed and kicks off his shoes. "God, it hurts to sit. Or stand. Or lay down."

He's reaching for his socks but with every inch he pulls forward, the mask of pain on his face gets more intense.

"Here. Let me." I drop to my knees in front of him and pat my thigh. He puts his foot up so I can pull off one sock then the other.

He stands and starts to unbuckle his belt. I glance away and stand too. "I'll just give you some privacy."

As I turn toward the door, his left arm reaches out to me. "Yeah, thanks." I take a quick peek back as his pants fall to the ground and he's left in just a pair of Calvin Klein boxer briefs. God, he's perfect. The hours he spends in the gym have been well spent. Muscles ripple and bulge over every inch of his body.

He looks over his shoulder at his back, straining to see the smeared blood. "This should be fun."

I turn around and step back to him. "Oh, right. Well, um, I can, you know, help with your back…if you want."

Dylan's eyes drop to my crotch and slowly trail up to my face. "Sure, if you don't mind."

I silently follow him into the bathroom. He turns on the bath faucet and sets the temperature. Looking down at his boxers then back at me, he steps over the side of the tub and lowers himself into the rising water, careful to keep his bandages dry. "Ahh, that fucking hurts but it feels good."

I reach for the bar of soap and unwrap the delicate paper surrounding it. Dipping it in the water with a hand towel, I lather it up. "Lean forward a little."

Dylan looks deeply into my eyes before scooting forward and resting his cheek on the side of the tub. With gentle strokes, I wash away the smears of blood on his back and side. When there isn't anything left on his back, I hold my breath and move the towel to the outside of his bronze bicep.

One eye peeks open and Dylan smiles faintly without stopping me. "I could just fall asleep."

"Well, I probably can't lift you out without hurting your shoulder so try to stay awake for another minute." With much more force, I run the sudsy towel over the front of his torso, stopping about an inch from the waist band of his wet boxers.

As soon as all visible traces of blood are gone, I drain the tub and help my sleepy savior out of it. I pat the drops of water from his glistening skin almost blindly because every time my eyes linger for more than a second or two, I find myself leaning into him. I want to lick the droplets off his body and then soil him again with droplets of my own. But I can't think that way.

Dylan has dealt with too much in the past eight hours and he just needs rest. "Here, you can wear this." I hold open the thick robe and case the arm of his bandaged shoulder into the right hole.

"Thanks." He turns his back and slides his left arm into the other sleeve. Just as he inches the fabric up his back, his towel drops, pooling around his bare ankles.

I want to turn away but I can't. After the robe is tightly closed, he turns and just stares at me. His gaze locks on mine and I don't know if I should kiss him or walk away.

I want to pull the string that's responsible for hiding his gorgeous body but I take a deep breath and a step back. "I'll make sure the front desk knows you're welcome to stay as long as you want." I fish a business card out of my pocket and drop it on the dresser. "If you need anything, just give me a call. I'll be on a plane at eight but you can call anytime and I'll get back to you."

Dylan just nods without breaking eye contact. "I don't even know what to say."

I smile and reach out to give him a half hug on his good side. "I know what to say." My palm cups the back of his neck and I tilt my forehead down to rest on his. "Thanks for saving my life. I owe you one."

He laughs and pulls away. "Well, this suite makes up for it. I'll be out of here by Sunday. I just need to get some shit in order before I do anything permanent."

"Take your time." I nod and edge closer to the door. "Take care of yourself, Dylan."

"Yeah, you too, Spencer," he whispers as I turn and leave the room, shutting the door quietly behind me.

Chapter Four

Dylan

Take care of yourself? What the fuck is that supposed to mean? If that isn't a blow off, I don't know what is. He says it like I'm never going to see him again.

Whatever. If he's coming to his senses, that's probably best case scenario for both of us. My life is in chaos and Spencer lives a thousand miles away. Other than a quick fuck, there's nothing for us. And Spencer doesn't seem like he's looking for a quick fuck.

Although I'm curious about what he is looking for, I let him leave. Maybe forever.

It's after two and I'm exhausted. I carefully recline on the bed and close my eyes. I don't bother to take off the robe because the thick cotton feels good against my mostly hairless body. My thoughts drift to the moments back at the apartment when Spencer held me against his body, cooing reassuring words in my ear. His warm breath smelled of mint and I wanted to suck it in. If it wasn't for the burning pain in my shoulder, I might have. And now he's leaving me.

I drift to sleep with thoughts of his hands on my body in the hot bath. I don't realize the stroking fingers along my rigid cock are my own until my eyes crack open and I'm alone. Both my legs are spread across the large bed and the robe I slept in is completely open.

Too far gone to stop, I reach down to cup my balls before I notice the bedroom door is open. I freeze for a moment and listen for sounds of Spencer but one glance at the clock confirms I'm alone. It's almost ten and he had to leave early.

Next to the clock is a bottle of water and some Motrin. I know those were there when I fell asleep and the door definitely wasn't open. Spencer came in before he left. Was I as exposed as I am now? I must have been. Well, if he still walked out then at least I know he's not that into me. At least not enough to stay.

It takes me another twenty minutes to get the energy to sit up and take a Motrin. There's a note under the bottle that I didn't see earlier.

Joey wants to talk to you.

-Spencer

The neatly written phone number must be Joey's so I reach for my phone and call him up.

"Hello," a soft voice asks. I recognize it as Joey's immediately.

"So, tell me why you tried to get me killed yesterday?"

I'm trying to be funny but by the sharp intake of breath on the other end of the phone, I know I missed the mark.

"Dylan, I'm so sorry. I didn't—" Joey's voice is shaking as he apologizes once again.

"Joey, babe. Relax." I lean against the cushioned headboard. "I'm kidding. But I do want to hear the story about how that all happened."

"Where are you? Are you still with Spencer?" I can hear a muffled voice in the background talking to him but can't tell what he's saying.

"Yeah." I smile at the mention of Spencer's name. "Uh, actually no. He's letting me use his hotel room for a few days but he had to go home or to work or something."

"Can we meet you for lunch at noon?"

I look at the time. "Yeah, I can do that. I'm moving kinda slow but I'll be ready in an hour or so." I throw my legs over the side of the bed and stand. "Um, actually... My car is still at the apartment. I should go get it."

"We'll meet you at the restaurant in the hotel then drive you to your car."

"Yeah, okay. I'll be down there at noon." I walk to the back of the room and yank the drapes open. It's a rare sunny day and the warmth radiates off the floor to ceiling window. Standing completely naked in the window is probably not the smartest thing to do in Downtown Portland but I don't care.

When I finally turn to the dresser, the bag from the hospital is gone and in its place are black sweats and a Stanford t-shirt. I lift the shirt to my chest and a pair of neatly folded white underwear shake loose.

Of course he wears tighty whiteys.

It takes a minute and several deep breaths to get the shirt over both arms and positioned snugly across my chest but it's better than wandering down to the gift shop in a bathrobe.

The sweats are a little long and a bit snug in the thighs but they work. I'll go shopping after I pick up my car.

I sit on the couch in the living room and turn on the TV. As expected, there isn't anything about Topher on the news but I know I can't ignore the situation for very long.

~**~

When I walk into the Daily Grill, I see Joey sitting in the middle of the room at a square table. The guy he was with at the apartment is sitting next to him, holding his hand on the table.

The restaurant is nicer than appropriate for tight sweats and an even tighter t-shirt but I ignore the glances my way from the hostess and servers. I walk straight through to their table.

Joey spots me as soon as I'm past the entryway and stands up. His arms wrap around my waist and I can feel his quiet sobs against my good shoulder.

"Hey, Joey. I'm okay." I lift my right arm so it's at a ninety degree angle. "See, everything still works. It was barely a surface wound."

"It could have been worse," he mumbles then steps back, into the chest of the man he was sitting with. "I'm so sorry."

"Okay, seriously." I grab his small bicep and give him a shake. "No more apologies. I'm fine and we're free. At least that's what Spencer told me…so this should be a celebration."

"I'm all for that." The man smiles and holds his hand out to me. "I'm Steve, by the way."

"Good to meet you, Steve." I shake his hand then we all sit down. I end up in the chair next to Joey and across from Steve.

"So," I pick up the menu, "I don't know about you guys but I'm fucking starving."

"Me too." Steve picks up his menu. "But I always order the cheeseburger so I don't even really need to look."

I chuckle and put my menu down. "That sounds good to me."

"Three cheeseburgers it is." Joey drops his menu and waves discreetly to our server to get her attention.

After ordering, I glance around the room to make sure I don't recognize anyone then I turn to Joey. "So, what's the deal with Topher? Can I go get my stuff or should I stay away?"

Joey looks to Steve just as he's taking a drink of his Coke. Steve swallows then says in a low voice. "Bobby said the debts are forgiven but you probably need to check in with Sal. He's in charge now."

I nod. I know that's the next logical step but I hoped Steve would have a better plan. "Yeah, that's what I thought."

"Sal's a good guy." He rests his hand on top of mine. "He's helped me out of a few jams and I know he's got your back. You just need to make sure he knows your intentions. If you just disappear, that could be bad."

"Disappear?" I look between the two men with a confused expression. "I'm not going anywhere.

This is my home. I don't have anywhere else to go."

"Well, either way. Just check in with him."

Steve and Joey drop me off in front of the apartment building where I was shot at one fifteen. I hop in my car then go straight to Macy's to pick up some clothes.

I'll probably never see any of my clothes again so I'm gonna need everything but for now I just need something that won't make other guys want to kick my ass. I'm not in the mood to knock out an innocent.

As soon as I'm done shopping for some essentials and changing into clothes that fit, I drive straight to Choppers.

I've never been inside but I know where it is. Topher was scared of his uncle, always worried Sal would decide to become a more vocal partner in the arcade and whore house the family ran. I've only met Sal a few times but he is a scary dude.

The parking lot at Choppers is like a Harley showroom on one side and a rodeo on the other with a line of big trucks. My Lexus CT200H sticks out like a sore thumb as I pull into a space between an F350 work truck and a battered pickup. Technically, my car belongs to Topher but he gave it to me when I started working for him and I don't think he'll be asking for it back anytime soon. It's just one more thing I need to work out with Sal.

It's early evening but dusk has settled as I walk into the dimly lit bar. All eyes turn to me as an outsider but no one stops me from heading straight to the counter in the back. I recognize a few faces from the apartment, including the bartender that has a beer waiting for me by the time I get to him.

"You could probably use this." He nods toward my shoulder. "Glad to see you up and around."

I accept the cold mug and take a drink. "Thanks."

"I'm Bobby, by the way." He holds out his hand. "You're Dylan, right?"

"That's me." I'm trying to keep my tone light but I'm in no mood for chit chat. I need to find out where I stand with the DeMonaco family so I can move on with my life...whatever may be left of it.

"You here to see Sal?" the man asks as he wipes a few drops of water from the counter in front of me.

"Yeah." I look around the room. People are still tracking my movements, although not obviously staring. Watching me without actually watching. "Is he around?"

"He's in the back. He expected to hear from you today."

I glance toward a hallway that must lead to offices. "Should I just head back?"

Bobby nods. "He already knows you're here. You can just go on in. Third door on the left."

I take a minute to finish off the beer then leave the empty glass on the counter. "What do I owe you?"

"It's on me. We're just glad you and that computer guy are okay."

I nod and head toward the back.

The third door is closed so I knock twice. It only takes a few seconds for the door to open wide and Sal's large body to fill the opening. "Dylan, my boy. It's good to see you."

He gives me a half hug on my left side then ushers me into his office. "Have a seat."

The room is not decorated for entertaining. It's purely functional with a long table that doubles as a desk. There's a laptop set up at one end with a leather desk chair so I pull out a smaller chair to his left. "Thanks, sir."

"Please, call me Sal. Or Uncle Sal." He looks almost sad as his gaze flits to the window. "Don't think I'll be hearing that very often anymore."

"Okay, Sal." I straighten up and turn so I'm fully facing him. "I'm here to find out what happens to me now. Is Topher coming back? Do I still have a job?"

"My nephew will not be back, son. I'm sorry about that." He lowers the lid of his laptop and steeples his thick fingers together. "But I do still need someone to run the entertainment businesses."

I love when people describe the whorehouse as an entertainment business. They should just say what it is. An upper class male brothel run by a crime family. See. Not so complicated. But, I just nod, waiting to see where he's going next with the conversation.

"I understand you are familiar with the day-to-day operations. You know who the vendors are and how to keep the boys in line?"

"Yes, sir. Sal." Maybe my college degree will finally come in handy. "I've been helping with some of the management of both places...but you should know that I owed Topher some money."

"Everyone owed that kid money." Sal shakes his head slowly then smiles. "Consider the debt paid. You'll be on the payroll now as the arcade general manager."

"That sounds great." This is exactly what I wanted when I took the job in the first place. "I really appreciate the opportunity."

"Yeah, well, I don't want to deal with that place. Too much drama."

"Yeah, there certainly is a lot of that." I laugh quietly. "What about Topher's apartment?"

"What about it?"

"Well, I've been living there for the past few years." I don't want to push my luck but I do need a place to stay so I go for it. "Is someone else moving in or is it okay if I stay there?"

Sal leans back in his chair and looks me over. His scrutiny makes my skin itch. He's one intimidating motherfucker.

"Yeah, sure." He leans forward and rests his elbows on the table. "You can stay there. You should stay close by in case of emergencies."

We discuss the details of my salary and the expectations of the job for a few more minutes before I feel confident that I'm not going to be shot in the back by another DeMonaco.

"Great." I stand up and offer my hand again. "Thanks again, Sal."

Sal stands and grips my left shoulder. "I know I can trust you, Dylan." His dark eyes penetrate mine as his words make my blood run cold. "You didn't protect my nephew in the end but I know that's because he went off the deep end and needed to be stopped."

I can only nod at the way he's presented my betrayal to Topher.

"But, I expect you to protect me and my family with your life, the same way you did for that computer guy." His small smile is the only indication that he isn't truly angry.

"Of course, Sal." My eyes drop to the floor. With everything that happened, I haven't given much thought to how it would look to Sal that I chose Spencer over my boss. "I swear I didn't know what was happening. By the time it started to make sense, I had a bullet in my back."

"I know, son." He squeezes my shoulder tightly. I want to flex the muscles under his grip but that could be seen as an act of defiance so I just let him dig into my skin. "But I expect complete loyalty and dedication going forward. I'll be fair to you and I expect you to have my back."

I don't even hesitate as I meet his stare and nod once. "You have my word, sir."

"Good boy." He steps back and takes his seat, dismissing me from the meeting.

I walk to the door but before I open it, I turn back one last time. "Sal?"

"Yeah."

"What about the, um, import side of the business?"

He smiles and looks up at me.

"I'll have my crew here take care of that. We'll let you know if we need any of your assistance but I want you to focus on the games and the boys."

"Got it." I'm not surprised Sal is going to handle the drug trafficking personally. That's more his style and his crew has been making runs for years.

Chapter Five

Spencer

I don't even know why I left this morning. The entire day has been completely unproductive. I can't concentrate on emails that I'm supposed to return or proposals I'm supposed to approve. I don't even realize I'm hungry until Barbara, my admin, drops a turkey salad on my desk.

The entire time I'm eating and trying to work, I keep picturing Dylan. I just wanted to leave some clothes where he would find them before he tried to get dressed. But when I walked in and saw him completely naked with his hand on his thigh and his cock resting next to it, I wanted to take it in my mouth.

He's so beautiful and so completely out of my league but standing over him as his muscular chest steadily rose up and down was too much. I'm not usually a voyeur but I couldn't look away. My cock instantly grew to full length as my eyes traveled from his slightly parted lips to his sculpted pecs down his washboard abs to his beautiful shaft.

It took every ounce of self-control to not pull out my dick and jack off right above him. But I didn't. I gave myself a firm rub through my slacks then left the clothes and Motrin I had the concierge deliver early in the morning.

By the time six p.m. rolls around, I give up the charade of working and head home, calling Steve from the car.

"So what's our next mission, Lois?" I ask when Steve answers his phone. He always teases me about looking like Clark Kent and after our little sting operation, I almost feel like Superman. Of course, Superman wouldn't have let an innocent man take a bullet for him.

"Hey, Spence." Steve is out of breath. Wonder what he's been up to? "Glad to hear you're in good spirits."

"Well, things could be worse." I clear my throat. "So, everything okay with you? The cops give you shit about anything? You know I can send one of my lawyers up there if you need one."

"Thanks, man, but I think we're okay. I'll let you know if anything changes."

"Good." I nod to myself, trying to sound aloof but knowing it's not going to sound that way. "So, um, have you heard from Dylan? I told him Joey wanted to talk so he might call."

Steve laughs quietly. "Yeah. We've heard from him."

That's it? Asshole is gonna make me beg. "So, he's feeling okay?"

"Yeah, he's okay. Took some Motrin and looked good when I saw him. That Stanford shirt looked a little snug...and familiar."

"You saw him?"

I can hear his smirk through the phone. "I did."

Whatever. I shouldn't be asking anyway. It's not my business. Dylan's feeling good so that's all I need to know.

"Cool. Well, I should let you go." It's my turn to laugh. "You sounded a little busy when you answered."

"Are you sure you don't want to know anything else?"

"Nope. Just wanted to check on everyone."

"Well, *everyone* is fine but you can call *everyone* yourself, you know."

"Yeah, whatever. I'll talk to you later, man."

"Later."

I don't want to call Dylan. It'll seem weird. He probably already thinks I'm some perv for going into his bedroom when he was sleeping…naked. No, I definitely don't want to call him. I don't even have his number. If he wants to talk, he'll have to call me.

~**~

Saturday and Sunday come and go without even a text from Dylan. I try to catch up on work I missed during the week but I'm still distracted by those grey eyes that pierced my heart with every intense gaze and sexy stare. I check my phone religiously to make sure I didn't miss a call but one never comes. Just silence and random work requests that mean a hell of a lot less to me than they did a week ago.

But, meaningful or not, life goes on. I've got a major release in less than a month and I need to focus. I throw myself into work. Writing code, testing revs and responding to partners is how I usually spend my weekends. This is no exception.

I'm on a conference call with China at eight thirty on Sunday night when a text alert dings on my phone. The number is unknown but my heart skips a beat when I read the message.

Chapter Six

Dylan

Walking back into Topher's apartment is a blessing and a curse. I've always loved this place and living there rent-free is amazing but I'm not sure how the rest of the staff will take the change of management.

I find Andre and Georgie watching a movie in the media room. Their reactions are mixed. Andre looks relieved to see me but Georgie's face falls.

"Where's Topher?" Georgie asks, sitting up straight in the leather recliner. "He was supposed to be back yesterday."

I take a deep breath then walk to them. "Topher isn't coming back."

They both look shocked but their fear is evident. "What do you mean?" Andre is quiet and thoughtful so he'll need some time to process things.

"Uncle Sal found out he was selling the paintings without sharing with the family. He dealt with him." I look at them each for a few seconds to make sure my words are sinking in. "Sal asked me to help out with the business for a while."

Andre nods and looks back toward the movie. I know he's not interested in what Seth Rogen would do during the apocalypse but I give him space to think.

Georgie isn't as introspective. "What the fuck does that mean? What happens to us?"

He stands up and starts to pace the short aisle.

"It means you're free." I smile tentatively, trying not to be callous. Topher was mostly a good man and did take care of us in his own way. I'm happy to be free but I'm not happy he's dead...or where ever he is. We didn't always want to be there, but if anyone really wanted to leave, they could have. Like Joey did. "Consider your debts paid. You can do whatever you want now."

"You're not serious." Georgie stops in front of me. "We can't just walk away. Who said so?"

"I say so." I take his hand and squeeze it. "I'm in charge and you're free to leave, if you want. Of course," I look up at Andre as I'm speaking, "if you want to stay on in the arcade or stable, you'll get paid like everyone else."

Andre looks me in the eye and slowly smiles. "Yeah?"

"Yeah." Andre is an amazing artist, able to forge almost any contemporary masterpiece he comes across. When he showed up on Topher's doorstep with an application to work in the arcade six months ago, no one was more surprised than me.

Topher and I grew up with his older brother, Mateo, but lost touch in high school. When Andre asked for a minimum wage job because he dropped out of high school the day he turned eighteen, just a few months shy of graduation, we took him in. He didn't have the same kind of debt the rest of us owed Topher. Andre just wanted food and shelter and protection from his psycho dad.

He got that in exchange for painting. He didn't participate in the group sessions with the other guys when Topher was high and looking to party. I'm not even one hundred percent sure he's gay. Truthfully, I don't think he's even lost his virginity. But, I'm not going to judge him for what I think he is or isn't. He can decide to stay or go.

Georgie is a different story. He's as flamboyant as they come and will choose silk panties and leg warmers over a pair of jeans any day of the week. I don't have to wonder about his decision for very long.

"If we join the stable, do we have to move into an apartment downstairs or can we stay here?"

Of course that would be his biggest concern. Whether he'd be booted from the penthouse. "You're welcome to stay up here." I cough, suddenly feeling weird over the situation. "I'm moving into Topher's suite but the other bedrooms are open. You guys can figure out how you want to divi up the space."

"Dibs on Joey's room." Georgie drops into Andre's lap, shocking him.

"Yeah, whatever you want." Andre awkwardly taps his leg, silently begging him to get up. "I'm not sure what I'm going to do."

"You thinking of leaving?" I'm surprised Andre would want to go considering he showed up without a friend in the world.

He shrugs. "I don't know. Not sure what I could do here."

"Well, you came looking for a job with the games." I sit in the chair next to him. "I'll need an assistant."

He raises an eyebrow and looks pointedly at my bandaged arm. "Look where that got you."

Smart ass. "A legit assistant. You can focus on the games if you don't want to interact with the boys."

"Okay." He relaxes for the first time since I told him Topher wasn't coming back. "If you think I can do it, I'll give it a try."

"Cool." I stand and start to walk out then I remember something. "Oh, speaking of Joey. I saw him and he's good."

"Really?" Georgie is now climbing up me, bouncing against my wounded arm. "Where is he?"

"Easy, there." I twist away from his excited hand gestures. "That shoulder's a little banged up."

"Ooh, sorry, sugar." He steps off and waits in front of me. "So, where's Joey?"

"He's living with his boyfriend in town. He seems happy."

"Little Joey has a boyfriend?" Georgie flops over the back of a chair. "Do tell!"

"I just met Steve today but he seems like a good guy." I smile as I think about the way they looked at each other. I can't remember looking at someone with that kind of emotion…maybe ever. "They look like they're in love."

"Seriously?" Georgie shakes his head. "I can't picture him in love. He was always so damn shy."

Andre finally speaks up, causing us both to look over at him. "Good for him. He deserves to be happy."

I smile at Andre. "I agree. But he probably wants his clothes so maybe we can pack up his stuff when you guys change rooms."

Georgie nods his head. "I'm on it. I'm excellent at packing shit."

Andre barks out a laugh. "Yeah, I bet you are."

I can't hold back my own low chuckle. Georgie does it on purpose but we need that kind of levity in the house.

~**~

The rest of the weekend is spent reorganizing the apartment and explaining that Topher is no longer in charge to the rest of the staff. Not all employees come in on the weekends but enough do that the rumors are spread by breakfast on Sunday.

All weekend long, I've wanted to call Spencer. I kept myself in check by helping the boys rearrange rooms but I can't stop thinking about him. But too much is unpredictable for me to think about a relationship. There are plenty of guys around here if I need a fuck so that's good enough.

For the past few months, I haven't even been in the mood to fuck. With the exception of Spencer's hotel room, I've been too stressed to even think about sex. Now that the biggest stress is gone, I'm thinking about it constantly.

Andre is working on a painting that he can actually put his own name on when Georgie announces he's meeting with a client. The appointment system is completely automated and runs like any other ecommerce site. Clients schedule an appointment and pay for their services in advance then can add on extras as needed. The boys each earn a commission on their sales and keep all their tips after the 'overhead' is paid.

Overhead includes their furnished apartment, housecleaning and protection. Now that I'm not working strictly for Topher, I'll probably play a more active role in keeping them safe.

Our clients rarely get out of hand but it's not unheard of. And once word gets out that Topher isn't around, they may try to push some limits. That shit won't fly with me. If someone becomes a little to rough or doesn't abide by house rules, I'll be having a chat with them.

I'm finally hungry enough to make a sandwich when I give in to the nagging in the back of my mind. Spencer's business card has been in my back pocket since I left the hotel, getting transferred from pants to pants. I've been telling myself it was just so I could thank him but I already did that. There isn't much else I owe him. I just want to say hi. A simple text to a friend isn't a big deal. Is he a friend? Maybe an acquaintance. An acquaintance that's seen me naked.

Hey. You get home okay?

I don't expect an immediate response. It's Sunday night and he's probably busy but my phone beeps before the screen even has time to dim.

I did. How's the shoulder?

I smile at his instant query about my welfare. It's nice to have someone care so much about how I feel and if I'm in pain. He's definitely a friend.

Fine. The Motrin helps. Thanks for that.

Sure. You still at the hotel?

Oh shit. He's been paying for an empty room for two days.

No. Back at my old place. Got my job back with a promotion.

That's great. You still a bodyguard?

I don't even know what to tell him. I should just be honest. I'm not ashamed of what I do. Well, not very ashamed. But I don't know if it'll scare him off. Actually, it's better to get everything out in the open right at the beginning. If he has a problem with my place of employment, it's better to know that now.

No. Managing some of the family businesses.

Does the uncle know?

Still worried about me. It's actually very sweet.

He's the one who offered me the job.

So you'll manage the art stuff?

The truth isn't my go-to response but I'm gonna give it a shot.

No. They also have a few entertainment businesses.

Instead of the instant response I've been getting, there's nothing for a good ten minutes. I've already put my phone on the nightstand and flipped on the TV when it finally dings.

What kind of businesses?

They own a building downtown that operates an arcade on the ground floor. I'm living in the pent house.

He's not stupid. I know he's gonna want more. If I don't fess up, he'll get it from Steve or Joey.

The arcade is one business. What are the others?

As soon as that text comes through, I get a follow-up.

Maybe I would be interested in investing?

LOL. I doubt that. It's a male brothel. Well, there it is. I've laid the truth out on the line. He can decide what to do with it.

Seriously?

Yup. I'm the general manager of both entities. Should be interesting.

And illegal. And dangerous. I'm not sure how to respond to him so I don't.

Again, a follow-up text comes a few seconds after that one.

And none of my business. Sorry. If you're excited, that's great.

Despite the 'products,' it'll be great business experience.

Is that why you're doing it?

Yeah, that and I need a job and a place to live. And, walking away after what I know is probably not an option so...I'm rolling with it.

I have to laugh at how calm and rational my words sounds despite the knot in my gut that is telling me I'm ruining something that could be amazing.

On the other hand, I can't ruin something that doesn't exist so I'll give him an out and move on.

I just wanted to thank you again. Have a good night.

Good night, Dylan.

CHAPTER SEVEN

SPENCER

A male brothel? Of all the things he could do for a living, I'm not sure there is anything worse. Okay, some things are worse but this is pretty high on the list. I don't even know how to respond. I knew from the minute I met him that we came from very different worlds that would probably never intersect naturally. But I had no idea what kind of world he truly came from.

I should have asked him to elaborate on his role. Is he a prostitute? He said general manager but I have to wonder what that entails. But like I said, it's not my business. He's not my boyfriend and this was his job before I met him. I have no right to comment.

I assumed he was just a bodyguard but I guess that's naïve. As usual, I look at people through my own filters and don't consider how they might be different.

Just because I grew up in an upper middle class neighborhood in Cupertino, California, birthplace of the personal computer and the company that gave me my start in programming, doesn't mean everyone else had that same upbringing. I'm tempted to do a Google search to see what comes up for him then I realize I don't even know his last name.

Talk about a slap in the face. The reality is, I don't know him at all. I just happened to be standing in front of him when he took a bullet to the back. Despite the fact that the bullet was meant for me, I still know nothing more than he used to work for an asshole and now he runs a whorehouse. That should be all I need to know to stay the fuck away.

But it's not. My mom always says I'm too curious for my own good. This is another example of me sticking my nose where it doesn't belong because I'm bored. And lonely. But mostly bored. But pretty damn lonely.

It's nine thirty when I call Steve. He answers on the first ring.

"Hey, Steve. Were you expecting my call?"

"Kinda." He laughs. "Joey is talking to Dylan right now."

"He is?" I sit forward and spin my chair so I'm facing the woods behind my house. "About me?"

"Why would it be about you?"

Indeed. Why would he be talking about me? No reason at all...unfortunately. "Oh, sorry." I don't mean to mumble but when I'm nervous, I either stutter or jam my words together. "I was just, uh." Damn. Hearing that Dylan is practically within earshot of the conversation changes everything. I don't know what to say without sounding like a crazy person.

"Babe, invite him over for dinner on Friday." Steve is talking to Joey before he returns his attention to me. "Sorry, Spence. You were saying?"

"Nothing." What was I saying? I can't just ask for his last name or anything. Can I? "Actually, I wanted to make sure Dylan's health insurance covered his expenses."

"His health insurance?" The disbelief in his voice is apparent. "That's what you're going with?"

"Wh-what?" I clear my throat and start again. "I know his job in, what did he call it? Oh yeah, *entertainment*, might not offer full medical coverage. So, I figured I'd help take care of the costs. He did save my life and all."

"How very noble of you." Steve's outright laughing now. He can really be an ass sometimes. "Well, it seems he'll be here for dinner on Friday. Why don't you join us and ask him yourself?"

"He'll think I'm stalking him." Which I am. "Just ask if he has insurance. If he doesn't, get me his last name and I'll take care of the rest."

Steve snorts then I hear rustling on the phone. "What's Dylan's last name?"

What? Shit! "Dude, don't be so obvious."

"Spencer wants to know." He's not trying very hard to muffle the speaker from his conversation with Joey.

"Asshole!" I shout through the phone. He's doing this on purpose to embarrass me...and it's working. I'll never be able to face Dylan again.

"Abraham. Why?"

"Huh?" I'm getting lost in my thoughts again.

"He wants to know why you asked."

Oh, Dylan wants to know why. "I told you. To help with his medical bills." As I'm talking, I'm pulling up a Google window and typing in Dylan Abraham.

There are over a million hits on the name but the first two pages don't have anything that seem relevant to my Dylan. Not *my* Dylan…but the Dylan I've met. Twice. Shit, where the hell has my perspective gone???

"Right. So should we tell him you'll be here on Friday?"

"No!" I not going to ambush the poor kid. If he wants to talk more, he can invite me over. "Thanks but I think I have an engagement that night."

"Sure you do." Steve knows me better than I'd like to admit. "Well, lover boy, I should get going. The offer's open if you change your mind."

"Thanks, man."

"Later."

~**~

The next few days are similar to the weekend. The only difference is now I'm not just wondering how Dylan is feeling and what he's doing for work. I've also got pictures of him supervising orgies and kicking the shit out of perverted business men in my head.

I want to get over whatever hero worship thing I've got happening but the harder I try to not think about him, the more obsessive I become. I've clicked through at least a hundred pages of search results for his name and none have given me anything useful. I did find a mailing address in Portland but that's it. Either he has zero web presence or he shares an extremely popular name with men much more social than he is. I curse myself for hoping it's the latter.

Feeling guilty for my covert cyber surveillance mission, I call the hospital Dylan was at and leave my credit card number. Insurance or not, I don't want him to be saddled with that burden. He was the only innocent person in the room and he's already paid too much for that pathetic plan.

By Wednesday at lunch time, I can't avoid the urge any longer. I send him a quick text.

Hi. How's it going?

Fine. But you probably know that already, don't you?

What? I hate texting because I can't tell if he's joking or pissed. Is he mad I asked Steve about him? Should I ask or act dumb…which isn't an act since I have no idea what he's talking about?

Um, I guess.

Need my social security number too? Wait, you probably have it by now.

Oh, he's pissed. Definitely pissed.

Can I call you?

Yeah.

I get up and close my office door as I hit the call button. He picks up on the third ring, breathless with a lot of background noise.

"Spencer."

Just hearing him say my name makes my dick twitch. The raspy whisper is how I imagine he sounds when he's about to come. God, it's hot.

"Hey, I'm sorry for asking Steve about you." My mouth feels like it's stuffed with cotton but I keep going. "I just wanted to help with your medical bills and I didn't know if you'd accept it so I figured it was easier to do behind your back."

That sounds much worse than I meant for it to sound.

"I can pay my own fucking bills."

"I know you can. You just shouldn't have to. You were innocent in the whole thing. I'm the reason you ended up in the hospital so I should pick up the tab."

"Thanks, but no thanks." He's still breathing hard. If I didn't know better, I'd think he was having sex. Oh yeah, I don't know better. Maybe he is.

"Um, is this a bad time?"

I hear a loud clank in the background. "It's fine. I just don't like people snooping around behind my back."

"I know. I'm not usually like that. I just...sorry."

"Whatever. But next time you have a question, ask me yourself."

"Okay."

"Cool. I've got to finish my workout so I'll talk to you later."

"Okay. Bye."

He hangs up without another word. I hate when people are mad at me. Especially beautifully ripped men that are dripping in sweat from torturing their muscles to the brink of exhaustion. Damn, I need to get laid. It's been over a year and the dry spell is catching up to me. I'm more of a predator than I'd like to admit.

CHAPTER EIGHT

DYLAN

The iron plates bang violently against each other with every repetition but I have a lot of tension to unleash. I usually work out for an hour at lunch but today I've been at it for almost two and I'm still not ready to focus on work.

My mind is going in a hundred different directions and they all point back to Spencer Lowe. I can still see those turquoise eyes boring into mine when I was in that hospital bed. Those same eyes that carefully inspected my wet body as he washed away the remnants of my gunshot wound.

I wonder what those eyes did when he came into the hotel room and found me naked. Did he stare? Did he avert his gaze? Did he get excited? I know the answer to that because he was sportin' wood the entire time we were together. Just like me. Fuck!

I decide to call him back after work. I know his heart was in the right place and his interest in my background wasn't sinister. I'm a little paranoid since being shot but I know he's cool and I just have to focus on keeping the boys safe and the businesses running smoothly. I can do that.

~**~

When I get up to the apartment, Georgie and Andre are watching Breakfast Club with a bottle of tequila between them.

"Sit, Dylan!" Georgie calls me over as soon as he sees me. "You have to play with us. We're taking a shot every time someone says shit."

"Seriously?" I stand over them, deciding whether I should just take the bottle away or let them have their fun. "How old are you guys?"

"Shut up." Georgie waves me out of his way. "They just said it. That's number nine."

Georgie takes a chug straight from the bottle then passes it to Andre. Andre repeats the move but almost gags as it's going down. "I hate tequila."

I look to Georgie. "You trying to kill the kid?"

Andre looks up at me indignantly then throws back the bottle again and takes another swig. "I'm fine."

Great. Now I feel like an old guy buying booze for the neighborhood kids. I want nothing more than to go to bed but I drop into the armchair and reach for the bottle. A shot or two might actually do some good right now. May help me get to sleep faster.

I only get through three shots before Andre passes out and Georgie runs out of the room to puke. I toss a throw blanket over Andre and leave him on the couch. If my shoulder wasn't jacked up, I'd carry him to bed but he'll be just as uncomfortable there as he'll be here tonight. Once he's mostly horizontal on the cushions, I pull off his shoes and drop them to the floor. Georgie's on his own.

I didn't think much about Spencer for the past hour but now that I'm stripping out of my clothes and sliding into my cool sheets, I'm overwhelmed by the need to hear his voice.

I was rough on him earlier and I don't want him to think I hate him. I'm actually touched that he'd make such a generous offer. Before I can sober up, one hand is dialing while the other fondles my balls. I like to knead and squeeze just a little. It's a satisfying combination of sting and pleasure.

Spencer doesn't answer immediately. I'm about to disconnect when he finally picks up. "Hello."

"It's Dylan." I'm speaking quietly, like someone is sleeping next to me. It's a wonder he can even hear me.

"I know." I hear fabric rustling in the background but we're both mostly quiet, listening to each other breathe.

"I wanted to apologize for being an ass earlier."

"Don't." He's a little more alert. "You have every right to be upset. I'm sorry for not just asking you directly."

His voice is like silk as it caresses my whole body. I give a little squeeze to my balls before pulling my left hand up to circle the base of my shaft.

"You can ask me anything," I murmur. I'm breathing deeply into the phone when I realize he is too.

"Anything?" he whispers.

"Mm hmm." I can't even form words. My head feels foggy like I'm ready to fall asleep but I know I won't be able to until I get off.

"What are you doing right now?" I almost can't hear him but his tone is so sexy, I'm completely tuned into every sound he makes.

"Right now?" I smile to myself. "Are you sure you want to know?"

I hit the speaker button and set the phone on the pillow right by my cheek so my right hand is free to do some of the work.

"Yeah," he pants out.

"I'm stroking my cock." I'm just drunk enough to know that's a stupid thing to say while still saying it.

"Oh."

I laugh quietly. "Was that the wrong answer?"

"No. De-de-definitely not."

"You're fucking adorable when you do that."

"Stutter?"

"Yeah." I stick my finger in my mouth and suck noisily. "Can I ask you a question?"

"Yes." I can hear the hesitation in his voice and it only makes me harder.

"What are you doing right now?"

He exhales right into the phone. "The same thing."

"Yeah?" Fuck me. I've never actually had phone sex before but this doesn't seem bad at all.

"Tell me exactly what you're doing."

"Oh, um." He hesitates for a few seconds then clears his throat. "Well, I'm pouring a few drops of lube onto the tip of my dick."

"Yeah? I bet it's so hard."

"It is." He's panting again. "I can't remember when I've been this turned on."

"Well, if I was there, I'd take that hard dick into my mouth and suck every last drop out of you."

"Oh." His deep moan almost pushes me over the edge.

"Will you do something for me?" I know we're both close but I want to make this count.

"Sure." His voice is strained but he agrees.

"Lube up your finger and press it against your asshole."

His deep intake of breath lets me know he likes the idea. As soon as he mumbles that he's ready, I press my middle finger against my own hole.

"Okay, baby. I want you to press in with me. Just an inch. Let my cock feel how warm your ass is."

My own finger breaches my muscle ring and slowly stretches the tight space. It's been a while since anything has been in there but it feels so good.

His loud groan forces me to slide my index finger in too. "That's right. Feel me press further until I'm all the way inside you. My balls are resting against your smooth skin, tickling your flesh as my cock thrusts deep into you. Bumping up against that spot that you know I'm looking for. The one that will make you quiver in my arms."

"God, that feels good."

I'm about to come just hearing his breath speed up. "I know it does, baby. You're so tight around me. My big rod is completely filling you up. There's no more room as I slide in and out, pounding into you with each stroke."

"Yes, Dylan. More."

"You want more, baby?" I swipe my right hand over the beads of liquid at my tip and use it to lube my shaft. My fingers are fucking my asshole while I thrust into my other hand to a tempo faster than I've moved in a while. "I'll give you more. I'll fuck your ass hard until I can't hold it any longer then I'll shoot my hot cream into you. Filling you with my seed until it's dripping out. I'll stay inside you while my hand pumps your dick up and down until you can't take it anymore."

"Yes, like that." I can hear him fucking himself to my voice.

"You like that? You want me to run my finger over the tip of your cock and wipe up that drop that I know is there? You want me to lick it up so you're inside of me too?"

I bring my right finger to my mouth and lick a drop of my own come off it. "Mmm, Spencer. You taste so fucking good. I could eat your come all night. I want to suck it out of you until you're begging me to stop."

"Shit. Fuck." Spencer's long moans push me over the edge at the same time he lets go. My fingers flick my prostate as I thrust up into my fist, imagining it's his beautiful ass hovering above me.

"God, yes." Spencer is still moaning as the last milky ribbon lands on my belly. "You're really good at that."

I chuckle quietly. "You should see me in person."

His squeaky response makes my dick twitch again.

"That was pretty amazing." In the back of my mind, I wonder if that was a good idea but I don't care. It felt too good to be bad.

"Yeah." He's obviously a man of few words in bed. It's almost a challenge.

"I should probably let you get some rest." As much as I want to, I can barely stay awake. "And I'm sleepy."

"Dylan?"

"Yeah."

"Are you drunk?"

"A little." I laugh. "Good night, Spencer."

"Good night. And thanks, Dylan." He hangs up before I can respond. That's good because I don't know what to say. What do you say to someone who thanks you for phone seducing and fucking them? I don't spend much time worrying about it as I drift off.

CHAPTER NINE

SPENCER

What the fuck was that? Other than the most erotic moment of my life. I'm still in shock that I actually did it. On the phone. I've barely touched myself in front of another guy...much less masturbated to the point of climax. More importantly, Dylan initiated it. Ten hours ago, I thought he hated me and I'd never speak to him again.

There are so many things going through my mind as I step back into the shower I was just emerging from when he called.

I quickly rinse off under a cool stream then get back into bed. I check my phone then leave it close to my head as I fall asleep, hoping he'll call me for a repeat performance. Or even just a quick hello.

When my alarm goes off at five fifteen on Thursday morning, there are no missed calls and no waiting texts. Assuming he's asleep, I tie on shoes and go for a run up the hill.

The house I just bought in Woodside is on a hill set deep in the woods. I love pushing myself to the brink of exhaustion to get to the top then slowly working my way back down. I'm back home and in the shower by six.

When I walk into the office an hour later, Barbara has a steaming cup of coffee in her hand to greet me. "Morning, Spencer." She eyes me up and down. "You look good."

"Thanks." I take a sip and savor the bitter aftertaste. "You too."

"I mean, you look...different."

That's when I realize I've got a stupid grin on my face. I brush my hand over my mouth and literally try to wipe it off. "I had a good run this morning."

"Oh, well, good!" She's such a sweet woman. She's in her sixties but as sharp and energetic as any of the twenty-year-olds in the office. And a hundred times more loyal. She is one of the first employees I hired and still my favorite. I only found her because she used to work for my dentist until he retired. She's been a godsend.

"Drink up because you have a busy day. Barker wants you to review the contract today and give him an answer. The clock is ticking if you want this to happen."

"Thanks, Barb. Hold my calls for the next hour and I'll go through it now. If I wait, I'll get buried in other stuff and never open it." I walk straight through the open space to my office in the back.

My messenger bag feels empty once my laptop is out so I toss it under my desk then boot up. There are always a hundred emails waiting for me but Barbara color codes each message by priority. I start with the reds and work down the rainbow from there.

The contract looks good and I give my lead attorney, Jim Barker, the okay to proceed with the sale. A major online retailer has been trying to acquire my company since before the IPO and now I'm ready to move on. I started building this app with photos of my friends in various club clothes and it's now the leading fashion inspiration app on the market. We went public last year and have doubled ad sales month over month for the past three.

I love Styleopia but I'm ready to move on. I have a few business ideas brewing that I'm ready to pursue but I won't have time until I pass the baton here. If all goes well, I could be fully out by the end of the year.

The day passes quickly without any word from Portland. Does Dylan regret calling me last night? Does he even remember it? I should have shut him down when I sensed he'd been drinking but once I heard his sexy voice whispering to me, I couldn't do anything but throw my head back and enjoy ride. And what a ride it was.

On Friday morning, I make the decision to take Steve up on his offer. Instead of calling to confirm, I decide to surprise him. That also gives me room to back out if I come to my senses.

But I don't come to my senses and at two p.m., I'm boarding United's non-stop to Portland. While waiting for everyone else to board, I call to book a room at the Westin even though I'm hoping Dylan will invite me back to his place. The ball is in his court. I'm going to show up at dinner. It's up to him to decide what happens from there.

My stomach is in knots from the moment I slide into the rental car until I knock on Steve's door at seven thirty. Dylan was supposed to arrive at seven and if the pearl white Lexus in the driveway is his, he's already inside.

I can hear muffled voices and laughing inside but I'm too distracted by my own reflection in the door glass to focus on any particular voice. I'm wishing I would have worn contacts instead of my glasses when the door flies open and Steve's wide body fills the space.

"Spencer, my man." He pulls me into a hug. "You did change your mind."

"Yeah, yeah." I slap his back a few times. "I hope you don't mind."

"Of course not." He pulls me through the doorway. "I want you to get to know Joey. Follow me. Everyone's in here having a drink."

"Oh, speaking of." I stop Steve and push a bottle of 2006 L'Apparita into his hands. "This is for you."

He takes a look at the Castello di Ama label and whistles. "Fuck, man. I haven't seen a bottle of this since the IPO."

"Well, I figured if I'm going to show up unannounced, I should at least bring a decent merlot."

"You know you're always welcome, announced or not. The more the merrier." Steve has a funny look as he turns toward his living room and we walk in.

Joey stands from his perch on the end of the sofa and walks to us. "Hey, Spencer. I didn't get a chance to properly thank you for everything you did but..." His eyes twinkle with moisture as he closes the distance between us and gives me a tight hug. "I really appreciate it. You have no idea how grateful I am to you. I'll owe you forever."

The sincere embrace feels nice. I don't get a lot of physical affection so I just nod and hold him for a moment. He's just about my height but even slimmer than me.

"I'm glad I could help." I pat his back twice then pull back. "You and Steve can call on me day or night and I'll always come."

Steve leans between us and whispers so only Joey and I can hear him. "Now it's our turn to help you out."

Joey smiles and slides under Steve's arm.

Steve nudges me with his shoulder as I turn to the rest of the men in the room. I didn't know what to expect when I was finally face-to-face with Dylan again but I definitely didn't expect to find him sandwiched between two beautiful boys that barely look legal.

A kid with glasses similar to mine and hair about the same color is openly staring from Dylan's right while his left side is buried under the body of a kid with spikey hair down the center of his head, dressed in purple hot pants and a mesh tank. With his arm wrapped around faux hawk boy, Dylan doesn't even bother to stand when he sees me.

After staring for a few seconds and lifting his jaw out of his lap, Dylan finally straightens up enough that his lap dog is forced to scoot away.

"Spencer, hey." He holds his hand out to me as if we're business acquaintances. Oh right, we are. With the exception of his drunk dial phone fuck, I'm nothing more to him than the guy who got his boss killed...or whatever the hell happened to that dude.

"Dylan." I shake his hand once then pull back. "Looks like you're healing well."

"Yeah." He scoots half an inch away from hot pants and rests his elbows on his knees. "Almost good as new."

"Great." I should leave. Despite the even number, I'm clearly the odd man out here and I just want to hop on the first plane back to California.

I turn to Steve with an apologetic look on my face. He knows me well enough to read my expression. "Spence, can you help me in the kitchen?"

Before I can answer or bolt, he grabs my elbow and walks me toward the opposite end of the modest bungalow.

Once in the relative privacy of the far room, he turns me against his fridge and puts his hand on my chest. "Don't."

"Don't what?" I put my hand over his, not pulling it off but ready to if I don't like what he has to say.

"Don't panic." He takes a step back then looks over his shoulder to make sure we're still alone. "I know how it looks but Georgie is just his roommate and Andre is the painter. He brought them here as friends. That's it."

I give him an incredulous look. "I'm not stupid. There's obviously something going on with that femme kid. It's cool. We aren't together or anything. My calendar was free this weekend and I thought about your offer so I came. That's it. I'm fine."

"Don't bullshit a bullshitter." He grabs a tray of cut veggies and hands it to me. "I know why you came and it wasn't to see my ugly mug. Just relax and see how things go. I think there's something there."

Ha! I want to laugh in his face but my stomach is still unhappy. It didn't relax when I walked in. It did a couple more flips and tangled a few other organs with it just for good measure. I'm on the verge of puking when we walk back into the living room.

Dylan is standing near the window with a drink in his hand and Joey is now seated in the twink sandwich. That Topher dude definitely liked them young. And skinny.

Steve pours a double of bourbon and hands it to me. "Drink."

I nod once and take a sip. Damn. I don't drink hard liquor often so it burns going down. But I square up my shoulders then walk over to Dylan.

He's waiting for me when I get to him. His cheeks are redder than they were a minute ago as he takes a deep breath. "I'm glad you're here."

"You are?" My voice wavers in shock. I take another sip to try to gain control of my faculties. "I mean, Steve invited me a few days ago and I had a free weekend so, you know."

He's watching my mouth as I babble my ridiculous excuses. He knows as well as I do that I'm only here to see him.

He continues to watch my lips for a moment but when it's clear I'm done speaking, his eyes flit up to mine and he takes another drink from his glass.

Without breaking contact, he gives me a knee melting smile. "Either way, it's good to see you. Talking to you was great and all, but I was beginning to wonder if that call was just a dream."

Now it's my turn to blush as I think about it. "So you do remember? I wasn't sure..." *Since you never called back.* But I don't say that. He has no obligation to call me. I have to keep reminding myself that I'm a techno geek and he's a gorgeous young model surrounded by other gorgeous boys that sell their bodies. And he runs a whorehouse. I shouldn't have come.

I put the glass down on a side table and turn toward Steve.

"If you'll excuse—" I'm silenced by Dylan's hand on my forearm.

"Don't go." I look to him and then back at the two boys on the couch. They're both watching us even though Joey and Steve are obviously trying to distract them into giving us some privacy. And failing miserably.

I put my hand over Dylan's and hold it for a few seconds before turning to him. "I shouldn't have come. This is too weird. I promise I'm not a stalker and you don't owe me any explanations."

I try to slip away but his grip is firm and he just pulls me closer to his solid frame. "Come on,

Spencer. You came all this way. You might as well eat before you head back."

Steve and Joey have now given up the charade and are watching us. I hate being the center of attention and this is the worst kind because I'm acting like a whiny bitch. Because that's what I am right now.

I pat his hand and plaster on a fake smile. "Ye-ye-yeah, okay. I'm starved."

"Me too." Joey pops up and grabs the hands of his two comrades. "Everything's ready so let's do this."

Chapter Ten

Dylan

Seeing Spencer walk through the door took my breath away. In his glasses and little boy haircut, he puts off a sexy innocence that I can't ignore. I want to feel his lips on mine and run my fingers through his hair. I want to smell his neck and breathe in his scent...but I don't do any of that. I don't even push Georgie off me so I can stand and give him a proper hello.

With a shocked expression, I just sit and stare until Spencer makes his way to me. I heard Steve inviting him to dinner but Spencer didn't mention it when I talked to him. Not that I've talked to him at all in the past two days.

Nope, after calling him in the middle of the night and phone fucking him, I've been too ashamed to call him back. And since he never called me, I assumed he was pissed or not interested. But he's here, standing over me with those piercing blue eyes. They're looking straight into me and I wonder what he sees.

All I can think about is that he's right in front of me. Spencer. Is. Here.

I straighten up and shift away from Georgie, pulling my arm back into my lap. "Spencer, hey."

I hold out my hand and we exchange pleasantries but all I can hear in my mind is his sexy panting and moaning from the other night. Shooting his load while I told him what I wanted to do to him. Then I never called him back. Fuck, I'm a douche.

I wanted to call a hundred times over the past few days but for the first time in a long time, I was afraid of rejection. I still am. Spencer isn't like the guys I usually hook up with.

He's smart and sexy and runs some super successful dot com company. I don't really date but when I do meet a guy, he's usually some meathead from the gym or a tourist that stops into the arcade with buddies. I've never been with anyone like Spencer and I'm sure he's never been with someone that manages male prostitutes for a living. Just associating with the DeMonaco family in any way is bad for Spencer's professional reputation.

Hanging out with the boys would be even worse for him and the family. The press loves any kind of scandal and they would eat this shit up. I stand and refill my glass then walk to the bay window that overlooks the front lawn.

Through the reflection in the glass, I can see Spencer and Steve walk back in. He looks to the couch then quickly seeks me out. When he sees me by the window, he turns back to Georgie and Andre.

Joey has replaced me on the sofa but by the way Spencer's eyes keep flashing to my new roommates, I really wonder what he's thinking. Is he interested in one of them? Is he jealous? I'm contemplating this as he walks over to me with a drink in his hand.

After a few awkward words are exchanged, I can easily see the regret on his face. I just don't know what exactly he's regretting. Coming to dinner? Phone sex with me? Leading me on because now he's interested in one of the kids that works for me?

I don't know what he's thinking but when it's clear he's about to leave, I have to stop him. I reach for his arm and hold it, wishing it was bare so I could have just a moment of skin contact. But the long sleeved shirt isn't enough to hide the warmth I feel radiating from his lean body. God, I want to see it. Touch it.

"Come on, Spencer. You came all this way. You might as well eat before you head back." I don't let go, even when his soft hand lands on mine, covering it up.

His eyes are searching mine, looking for sincerity or regret and who knows what, but I guess he finds it. His awkward agreement makes me want to pull him to my chest and kiss those pink, full lips.

I want to assure him that trusting me is a good thing and I'll always protect his heart. But neither of those are true. The only thing I can say with sincerity is that I won't lie to him. As much as it might hurt us both in the end, I'll always tell Spencer the truth. I just hope that if he's going to smarten up and bail, he does it before my guard comes down completely. I'm already falling for this bashful geek and if I allow this attraction to go much further, I won't be able to let him go at all.

~**~

Steve and Joey have the dining room set up like a buffet with three pots of melted cheese surrounded by meats, veggies and bread. It smells amazing as we all grab a plate and start dipping various bite sized chunks into the simmering pots of gold.

"The first one is traditional Swiss." Joey points to the pot on the left. "The middle is a cream cheese and parmesan blend. And the one on the right is a Brie fondue."

They're all delicious. I can't remember the last time I ate a meal that wasn't shoved between two slices of bread or a bowl of cereal. The week was so crazy, I mostly survived on protein shakes or quick food as I was coming or going from the apartment.

By the way Georgie and Andre are shoveling food into their faces, I realize they aren't much better off. "Damn, I guess I need to start feeding you guys more often."

They nod and smile at the joke but I can feel Spencer's eyes on me as soon as the words are out of my mouth. I guess this is a good time for me to practice that telling the truth thing with him.

I clear my throat and run my tongue across my teeth to make sure there aren't any broccoli or carrot pieces stuck in them before I turn to Spencer. "I didn't properly introduce you to Georgie and Andre." I gesture to each as I say their names and they each look up and give a polite nod. I'm glad Georgie has a plate in one hand and a chunk of dripping bread in the other or he'd probably climb up Spencer's body and give him a 'nice to meet you' kiss.

"They work for me and are living with me in Topher's apartment." Not really wanting to explain more in front of everyone, I turn toward the boys. "Guys, this is Spencer Lowe. He's a friend of Steve's and is responsible for getting our debts...forgiven." Everyone in the room knows I really mean getting Topher *removed* from the family, but that doesn't need to be voiced.

Georgie's interest perks up a little more but it's Andre I'm watching. He's not taken his eyes off Spencer since he walked in and the look that seemed curious at first has taken on a deeper, more lustful stare. I know that stare because I've also had it since I met the tech genius.

I have to bite back the urge to tell Andre to back the fuck off because Spencer's mine. He isn't mine. He would actually be perfect for Andre. Andre is such a sweet kid that just needs to be loved and left to do his painting in peace. He's not like Georgie...or me. He wouldn't survive in the stable. If I was truly taking care of the kid, I'd encourage a relationship between them.

Spencer could give him the cultured and pampered life he deserves. The life he *needs*. But I'm not that altruistic. I want to be but just the thought of Spencer holding Andre in his arms the way he's held me, whispering into his ear the way he did after I was shot... No, I can't do it. Not yet anyway. I just want a little bit more time with the fantasy that he could be happy with me before I shove him into the direction he should go.

Chapter Eleven

Spencer

He needs to feed them more? What the hell does that mean? Is he a roommate or their guardian? They both look young but can't be *that* young.

Dylan is making a valiant attempt to avoid looking at me but I need to know what's going on. The mixed signals are giving me a headache. Well, it's that or the way I've been gritting my teeth since I saw that Georgie kid crawling all over Dylan when I walked in.

Regardless, if I'm staying, I deserve to know what I'm sticking around for. "So, you guys work with Dylan? What do you do?"

Georgie has an almost panicked expression as he looks to Dylan for guidance. Dylan shrugs and gives a slight nod. Georgie's shoulders relax a little as he licks some cheese off his pinky. "I just started as an, well, I guess the polite word would be escort, for Paddles."

"Paddles?" I can just imagine him walking around with a ping pong paddle, whacking the ass of sickos that can't get it up for their wives anymore.

Dylan finally makes eye contact. "Paddles is the arcade. That's the public name for both sides of the *entertainment* business."

I nod and offer Georgie my hand. "I see. Well, it's nice to meet you." I hope my smile doesn't relay the unease I feel about this pretty and extremely sexual young man living in the same apartment as Dylan.

I turn to Andre, the more exotic of the two. His dark eyes have been tracking me since I walked in and I can't tell if it's for a good reason or bad. Does he fear my presence in his life? Is he afraid I'll report his forgeries? Does he have a thing for Dylan?

All these questions race through my mind each time I glance at the boy and feel his intense stare.

"And what about you, Andre? Are you also an escort?"

I can feel Dylan stiffen up beside me, his normally casual stance stilled by my question.

"Um, no, sir." Andre looks down at his hands as he fidgets with his fondue fork. "I'm working as Dylan's assistant in the office."

"That's great." I offer my hand but it takes him a moment to notice it. When he does, Andre wipes his right hand on his jeans then gently takes mine. It's a timid shake that conveys nothing but the vulnerability this kid exudes. "And, please, call me Spencer. I'm not quite as old as I look."

He gives me a brief smile then pulls his hand back and stuffs it in his pocket.

"Andre, may I ask how old you are?"

Dylan's head jerks toward me and I can see the anger on his face in my periphery but I don't break eye contact with Andre. I'm not trying to imply anything illegal or immoral but if he's underage, Dylan may be doing more harm than good by taking him into his home and his business.

"I'm eighteen, sir." The way his voice cracks makes me feel like shit. I'm scaring the kid for no reason. If he ended up with that Topher guy, he had a good reason.

"Well, you'll appreciate your youthful appearance for many years to come." I smile and pat his arm. "It's really nice to meet you."

His cheeks flush and he quickly looks away, apparently not reassured by my comment. I'll have to do a better job of letting him know I'm here to help, not to interfere.

I haven't had much exposure to at-risk teens. And by much, I mean absolutely none. I grew up in a suburban town of overachievers that were raising a bunch of uberachievers. As part of that entitled-to-the-best-of-everything generation, it was easy to forget that life wasn't always so easy for people.

My parents will probably never approve of me being gay but they were willing to ignore my sexuality, or lack thereof, to make sure I was in all the important AP classes, joined the most impressive extracurricular clubs and finished in the top of my class at Stanford.

Andre definitely has a story and I'm curious to know it but tonight isn't the time or place. Tonight, I'm going to eat a deliciously fattening meal with an old friend.

The wine is flowing and after about an hour of chatting around the dining table and gorging ourselves on cheese, we all move back into the living room. I strategically sit in one corner of the sofa so there is only space for one person to sit next to me.

I can feel Dylan watching me but he stops at the bar to refill his glass instead of taking a seat. That's fine.

As soon as Dylan's back is turned, Georgie slides onto the cushion next to me. His thigh is pressed against mine, even though the rest of the long sofa is vacant.

"So, you're from California? I looove California." Georgie's hand is on the front of my knee. Not entirely inappropriate but I still can't help but seek out Dylan. His eyes are glued to Georgie's hand and he looks pissed. What I can't tell is if he's pissed at me or at Georgie. Or both.

"Yes, I was born and raised in the bay area. My office is in San Francisco but I live down on the peninsula. Do you know the area?"

His hand slides up just an inch so it's cupping the top corner of my knee. "I used to go to San Fran all the time but it's been years. Maybe I can go visit you sometime."

I have to laugh. "Yeah, maybe."

He leans forward and whispers in my ear. "And you know you can visit me anytime. I'll give you the friends and family discount."

"Uh, th-th-thanks." I can feel my face burning as I scoot away a few inches. "I'll k-k-keep that in mind."

"Refill time!" Georgie gives me a quick kiss on the cheek then jumps up, leaving me alone on the sofa. My own glass is still half full so I don't need to get up but I look around the room.

Joey is speaking to Andre but Andre's eyes are trained on me. It takes a few moments for him to notice I'm watching but when he does, his mouth pulls into a small smile before he looks down at his feet.

I can appreciate his shyness. He and I are practically the same person on the surface. But I can't even imagine how different we are on the inside.

While I'm lost in my thoughts, I hear the voice I've only been hearing in my dreams for the past few days.

"So how long are you in town?" Dylan is a few inches away in the spot Georgie just vacated.

"A night or two." I shrug and take a sip from my glass. "I didn't get a return ticket yet because I wasn't sure what my schedule would be."

"Are you in a suite again?" His demeanor is that of indifference but he keeps glancing at my face to see my reaction.

"No." I give a low chuckle and shake my head. "I only got that room to keep up appearances if your boss started nosing around. I just have a standard room."

Dylan nods and leans back. "I'm surprised you aren't staying here."

It was a valid point. In the past, I'd stayed with Steve a few times but now that he had a live-in boyfriend, I didn't want to impose. Joey is still speaking to Andre but Steve isn't with them. "Nah. They don't want me hanging around here."

"Of course we do." Steve's booming voice startles me as it vibrates through my ear.

"Ass." I laugh as he stands up and sits on the arm of the recliner next to me. "You know you're welcome to stay here. We'd love to have you."

"Yeah, I know what you'd love to have me for." Steve has a reputation for being a bit kinky and liking the shock factor of doing crazy things. "I can only imagine what you guys would do if I had a few drinks in me."

Steve laughs then looks over at Joey. "Maybe someday but we're not there yet. I'm not quite ready to share."

The adoring look he gives his new partner makes it clear he'll never be ready to share him.

Dylan is just taking a drink when the subtext of what we're talking about sinks in. He coughs up the liquid, spitting it across the room. All eyes are on Dylan when Steve lets out a guffaw that turns everyone's head.

"Joey?" Dylan looks over to the shocked kid at the other end of the room. "It really is always the quiet ones!"

Joey furrows his brow as he looks to Steve for reassurance. Steve stands and walks to Joey in three large strides. "Don't worry, little duck. He's just jealous."

Steve winks back at Dylan then wraps his arms around Joey, whispering in his ear.

The scene is sweet and I'm happy for my friend. He hasn't been truly happy during the entire time I've known him so to see him giddy in love makes me a bit sentimental.

"Seriously, you should stay here." Dylan looks over at Joey and Steve. "No sense being alone after coming all this way."

I shrug, internally debating how to respond. I don't want to sound hurt that he's clearly brushing me off but I can't keep my mouth shut. "I'm used to being alone."

He swirls the last drops of liquid in his glass, staring into it. "If you don't want to stay here, you can stay at my place. I'd like the company and we have plenty of room."

My heart is pounding as I contemplate his offer. I desperately want to say yes and follow him to his bed. But that might not be what he's asking.

"Is there?" I nod toward Georgie. He's thumbing something on his phone with a big grin on his face. He seems to sense my gaze because he looks up and winks. I have to look away because his pretty face reminds me of what Dylan goes home to every night. "Seems like you've already got a full house."

Dylan takes a deep breath and lets it out slowly. "I told you I'm their boss." He puts his hand on my shoulder, moving my attention back to his beautifully tanned face. "There's nothing else going on. I just feel an obligation to look out for them now that Topher's gone."

"Still. You have access to a lot of *company* if you want it." I know I'm being petty but I can't help the insecurity. He's the guy all guys want to be. He's got the perfect body. Perfect lips. Perfect skin.

"Maybe." His voice is low and seductive as he leans into my neck. "But I'd like *your* company tonight."

"You would?" I shouldn't go for it. Desperation isn't a good look on anyone but I really want to feel Dylan against me. His lips pressed to mine. His strong muscles holding me. "What about them?"

Dylan looks like he's starting to get annoyed. "What about them?"

"Nothing." I clear my throat and nod. "Okay, that sounds good."

He relaxes back into the sofa, rolling his neck so his face is close to mine. "Good."

CHAPTER TWELVE

DYLAN

It's stupid and unfair to both of us but I can't stop myself from inviting Spencer back to the apartment. My plan was to be cordial and maybe meet him for lunch on Saturday but with Georgie propositioning him and Andre eye fucking him all night, my possessive streak took over and I suddenly needed him in my bed.

That shit about Steve and Joey sharing him was too much. I'm not sure if it was a joke or not but I didn't like it.

I'm no prude and have been in several group scenes with Topher but Spencer seems too modest—too pure. He deserves complete attention and devotion from his lover. I can't do that long term but I'm damn sure gonna try for that tonight. Just one night. Maybe two if he can stay until Sunday.

After another hour of rushed chatting, we're able to excuse ourselves. "I'll ride with Spencer," I say to Andre, tossing him the keys to my car.

He nods and walks with his head down to the driver's side of my Lexus then climbs in. Georgie babbles animatedly into his phone while sliding through the passenger door.

I walk quietly beside Spencer to a black Camry parked on the curb. To my surprise, he opens the passenger door for me then blushes when I raise an eyebrow. I didn't peg him for a romantic but I probably should have.

With a little bit of fanfare to properly tease him, I glide in the leather seat and fold my hands in my lap. Looking up at him from underneath my eyelashes, I bat them a few times. In a high-pitched, southern belle accent, I ask, "Will you help me with the seatbelt, kind sir?"

"Shut up." He snorts out a laugh then slams the door as I wave my hand in front of my face like I've got *the vapors.*

Once Spencer is in the driver's seat, I give him a final rub before dropping the subject. "You do realize you'll be visiting a house of ill repute. You might want to pick up a disguise of some kind so the paparazzi doesn't see you walking in."

Spencer leans his elbow onto the center console. "Do you think I'm a prude or just a super nerd?"

I can't help myself. I shrug and with a straight face say, "Both."

He holds a tight smile for a few seconds before nodding curtly and straightening out. When he puts the car in gear, his face relaxes. "You're probably right."

"I think it's cute." I reach over and squeeze his hand that's resting on the shifter. "I like that you're a gentleman. And I like that I can tease you about it."

His look of feigned annoyance is priceless. "Great."

"So, tell me the truth…" I wait for Spencer to stop at a light so he can focus on me. "Why did you really come up today?"

He blows out a breath then glances at me before staring at his hands on the steering wheel. "You didn't call and I…"

The light turns green and he hits the gas. As if that is going to work.

"And you what?" I'm terrified by what he might say but also excited. I want him to say the words I've been feeling for over a week.

"I...kept thinking about you." A crimson hue spreads across his pale cheeks as his eyes dart from me to the road. "Then after that call... Well, I really wanted to see you."

"Turn right at the next light and it's the first driveway on your left." We're almost in the parking garage so I give his fingers a squeeze but don't say anything yet. I want to be looking right at him when we finish this conversation.

"Okay." Spencer is biting his lower lip, probably feeling self-conscious after his declaration but I don't say anything yet. Instead, I slide my thumb across his lip, gently pulling it away from his teeth.

"Park in the reserved space by the elevator." My words are barely a whisper but Spencer swallows and nods.

As soon as the car is parked, I jump out and walk around to the driver's side. Not wanting to wait another second to feel him in my arms, I open Spencer's door and pull him out.

He's shocked and maybe a little scared when I press my body to his, smashing him against the side of the car. "I couldn't stop thinking about you either."

I cup my palm around his neck and pull him toward me, kissing his full lips. Spencer is tense at first. Still unsure about my reaction to his words but with each pass of my mouth across his, he relaxes into me.

After a few more seconds, he's fully engaged, matching my mouth movements and adding his hands and hips. I can feel his erection through his jeans and I want to pull it out and worship it. Worship him. He's so beautiful when he's excited. And even when he's not.

When we're both panting for air, I pull back and trace the line of his jaw with my tongue, nipping his earlobe and licking along the length of it. "Let's go upstairs."

~**~

As we open the door to the apartment, Georgie appears dressed in a lime green sequins jumper and knee boots. I want to laugh as Spencer's eyes almost pop out of his head.

"I'm working tonight so don't wait up." Georgie pulls a white leather coat off the rack by the door then turns to Spencer and tickles underneath his chin with his pointer finger. "Well, you can wait up if you want, gum drop."

"Be careful, G." I don't have time to peel him off Spencer right now. We've got someplace to be. Namely, in my bed.

"Um hmm." He spins out the door and we're alone again. Well, almost alone.

"Andre?" I call out, knowing he's got to be around here somewhere.

"In the studio." His normally quiet voice rings out loud and confident when he's in his studio. It's the only place I ever see him really relaxed.

"Okay, we're going to bed."

"Good night," Andre calls out in a slightly less confident voice. His insecurity can only be matched by the mortification I see cross Spencer's face.

I pinch Spencer's ass to bring him back to the moment then whisper, "Oh, I plan to have a good night."

CHAPTER THIRTEEN

SPENCER

I feel like a fifteen-year-old virgin walking into, well, a whorehouse. I know Dylan isn't going to put me in any uncomfortable situations but I'm in completely foreign territory here.

I follow at Dylan's heels like a puppy but when we enter his bedroom, I start to panic. He's probably been with hundreds of guys. Well, at least one hundred and I've been with five. Five! And that's counting the two from high school.

The magnitude of my inexperience is overwhelming. Between my nerves and my awkwardness, I'm starting to feel dizzy. I rest my hand on the dresser while Dylan locks the door and steps into my back. His chin is the perfect height to rest on my shoulder.

When his strong arms wrap around my body, my apprehension and fear start to melt away.

"Are you okay?" he whispers against my cheek.

I nod, unable to trust my voice to not squeak.

"Are you as happy to be here as I am that you're here?"

I let out a deep exhale and rest my cheek against his. "Yes."

"Good. Then come relax while I make a few phone calls."

I let Dylan lead me to his bed and push me into a sitting position. He sits next to me and kicks off his shoes before pulling out his phone.

I'm not really sure what he wants me to do until he flops back and pulls me down with him so we're both laying across the width of his bed. His playful smile is back as he twists up and leans toward me on one elbow. "This'll just take a minute."

I nod and pull out my own phone, checking emails and trying to look casually busy. I'm not very good at it. Especially when his fingers dip into my hair and twist the dark strands around while his call connects.

"Hey, Josh. Everything okay?"

I can hear a man's voice on the other end of the line but not well enough to make out any words.

"How many on the premises tonight?" Dylan nods in approval at whatever he hears.

"Yeah?" His hand stills and he looks toward the ceiling. "You checked them out?"

"Okay, well, I'm in the building if you need me," he catches me watching him then winks, "but I'd rather not be disturbed if you can avoid it."

"I'll be down by nine tomorrow."

Dylan disconnects the call and tosses his phone to the nightstand.

I get bold and reach out to him, gently running my fingertips over his chest. "Is everything okay?"

"I think so." His eyes close for a second before he turns to me. "Can we talk business for a second?"

"Of course." Now this is something I can handle. It's not what I was expecting but at least I can speak and *act* confidently around this topic. "What's going on?"

"Probably nothing but this is all so new to me that anything out of the ordinary makes me nervous." His fingers begin tugging at my hair again and I almost purr at the comforting sensation.

"What's out of the ordinary tonight?" Seeing this strong and self-assured man on edge has me worried too.

"Josh got a call for a group tonight. Three guys we've never seen before. That in itself is unusual because people don't usually bring their buddies unless it's a divorce party or something. But they also wanted to be in private apartments...not in the suites where the guys usually work."

"Can you just say no?"

"We can but they're high rollers and are throwing around some big cash. I hate to take that away from the boys if everything's legit."

"Is everything legit? Do you do background checks or anything?"

Dylan lifts back onto his elbow so he's looking down at me. "Josh is head of security and he did a more thorough check than usual and everything came up clean. It's probably fine." His hand moves to my waist and gently pulls out the shirt I've got tucked in. "Anyway, I'm more interested in doing a thorough check of my own...right here."

Once the fabric is free from my jeans, Dylan's smooth fingers dance along my belly, raking through the dark hairs trailing down the center.

My muscles quiver under his soft touch. I want this moment to last forever but I also want to tear off my clothes and feel him touch me everywhere. Apparently a big ass tease, Dylan sits up and lifts his knee over my waist so he's straddling me.

I gasp at the sight of such a beautiful man looking at me with nothing but lust in his eyes. He breaks his stare only long enough to pull his shirt up over his head. Once his bare chest is displayed to me, I release a barely audible whimper at his perfection.

"We're uneven here," Dylan murmurs as he reaches for the lowest button on my shirt.

"Yeah, tell me about it." I'm about a two on the hotness scale and he's about two hundred. Not that I need the reminder.

His teeth bite into my chest before I even realize what happened. "That's not what I meant and you know it."

I have no idea what he did or didn't mean. All I know is that chomp into my left pec has my dick leaking and my heart pounding. "Sorry."

"What I meant is," he loosens another button, "you've seen me practically naked." Another button is released and Dylan places a light kiss on the corner of my lips. "Actually, you've seen me completely naked…"

His hands spread over my stomach and rub firm circles over my taut skin, leaving a trail of goose bumps everywhere he touches.

"And I haven't even seen you without your shirt yet."

Dylan's tongue slips between my lips and dances with mine, exploring my mouth then allowing me to take over and do the same to him. When the last button is free, Dylan drags my lower lip between his teeth and pulls away.

"So I need to catch up." Dylan's hands slide my shirt past my shoulders and under my back so it slides completely from my arms. Only my wrists are restrained by the buttons still holding the fabric to my body. My tense fists are hidden within the inside out sleeves.

I give him a pleading look but that only encourages his playful side. "You want it off? Hmm… I think this could be more fun."

With my shirt gathered up under my ass, my hands are held captive next to each thigh. I'm completely at his mercy and shivering with need. "Dylan…"

"That's right, baby. Say my name." Dylan's mouth is lavishing attention to my pecs, nipping at my skin in a way that makes me hypersensitive to each touch.

When he undoes the top button of my jeans, my hips buck off the bed, begging him to hurry. "You're killing me here."

"We have all night. I'm going to make sure I get my fair share of touching and teasing before my pants come off. In fact, I think I owe you a bath…"

"Now?" My voice is practically a squeak. I don't know if I can stand the torture of not being able to touch him back. Although, he'd have to release my hands in the bath…

"Good point." Both of Dylan's hands are around my hips, crawling beneath my jeans and underwear. He pushes them away from my skin then slowly moves them down my thighs. His mouth is hovering at my belly button. "We'll do that later. Right now, I just want to look at you in my bed."

He scoots off the back of the bed, taking my clothes with him. Everything except the damn shirt restricting my hands. With Dylan standing over me, inspecting my naked body, all sense of dignity is lost. I'm reduced to begging.

"Please, Dylan. Just... just do something." I wiggle my ass against his soft comforter. "Let me do something. I want to touch you...for real."

His devilish smile makes me tremble. He's got a plan and I know the torture is going to be much worse before it gets much, much better.

"Oh, but you have." His lips graze the tender skin inside my hips. "You've watched me slip out of my clothes. You've rubbed a wet towel over my skin, lathering me up while I sat helplessly in the tub."

"You weren't helpless." I breathe out then take a shuddering breath in again. "You could have touched me."

Dylan shakes his head as his tongue draws a figure eight on the inside of my left thigh. "I was still in shock over everything that happened."

His breath cools my wet skin, causing a shiver to pass over me. My cock is fully engorged, begging for attention from more than Dylan's clear grey eyes.

"Even then, I knew I wanted to do this slowly, when we were both fully engaged." He slides up my center, pressing my dick against his chest as he does. "Are you ready to be fully engaged?"

"Please." Dylan slides back down me. His scruffy cheek caresses my cock before he takes it in his mouth. He sucks hard from the first touch, slowly pulling my head in then moving down my length.

He doesn't take a breath as I hit the back of his throat and move into the tight canal. "Fuck!"

I can't keep my ass on the bed. I lift up and Dylan greedily accepts all of me. When he finally pulls back to take a breath, I'm able to breathe as well. He continues slow strokes with his lips and tongue while I ball my fists, trying to maintain control. Watching him raise and lower off my dick is the most beautiful sight I've ever seen.

He's a perfect creature and he's sucking my cock like a starving man would suck meat off a bone. Dylan's eyes alternate between watching my face to closed, as if savoring the moment. The look of pure enjoyment pushes me over the edge I've been teetering on for hours. Days, actually.

"Dylan, pull off..." I try to back away but he follows me as I press into the mattress.

As he sucks harder, I explode in his mouth, thrusting with each surge of endorphins that rush through my body. It feels like minutes pass before I am out of the clouds and back to reality.

"Shit, I'm sorry." I'm not but it seems like the right thing to say. "I tried to pull out."

"Why?" Dylan lifts his head up but is still close enough to tease my slit with his tongue. "You taste amazing."

"Really?"

"Fuck yeah. No one's ever told you that before?"

"Not really." I can feel the flush of my body transferring to my face. "I've never really done that in someone's mouth before."

"Their loss." Dylan slithers up my chest. After a moment of just staring, his mouth lands on mine then his fingers expertly release the buttons at my wrists. As soon as my hands are free, I grasp at his silky skin, tracing each muscle and pulling him fully against me.

With one hand holding Dylan's body against mine, I let my other hand trail down his spine and under his jeans. Discovering bare skin under his pants makes me almost cry out, fully hard again. Instead, I flatten my hand and slide all the way down his ass so my middle finger is resting against his hole. "I need to touch you."

"I'm all yours, baby." Dylan lifts away from me just enough to open his jeans and kick out of them. "Now what are you going to do with me?"

Everything. Anything. God, just looking at his beautiful muscles makes me want to shoot my load. "Can I lick you?"

His sexy grin turns excited. Dylan barely nods then crawls all the way up my chest so his hairless balls are hanging just above my mouth.

I take a deep breath to fully experience him. A hint of cologne is mixed with his own body scent and I want to bury my nose in the warmth.

Instead, I take a hesitant swipe at his sack. With my tongue flattened, I pull from left to right then right to left.

His balls are heavy as they rest against my lips before I delicately suck one then the other in. Swirling my tongue around the delicious orbs makes me want to never let them go but there is still so much to explore.

Both my arms wrap up his thighs, teasing his crack with my fingertips. After memorizing the shape and feel of his scrotum, I pull away and reach for his neck. When I've got a good grip, I nudge him downward so his cock is perfectly angled to enter my mouth.

I take him in slowly, pushing him through my tightly pursed lips without any suction at first. I just want to taste him. Memorize his texture. His silky skin is smooth as butter in my mouth. I haven't given a lot of blow jobs so I've never mastered deep throating but I do my best to fully envelop him in my hot wetness. Looking up through my eyelashes, I see Dylan staring down at me. His eyes are hungry so I close mine and focus on making him feel as good as he made me feel. Using only the limited experience I have, I close my lips around his head and suck. When Dylan moans and pushes in a bit, I take that as a good sign and press him closer.

Without losing suction, I pull off a bit and take a breath through my nose. After a few more strokes, I release him completely, wanting to drag this out a little longer. With my arms still hooked under Dylan's thighs, I scoot down until my nose is nestled under his balls again. He smells like a man. I love it. I burrow into his smooth skin for a moment before swiping my tongue across his hole. He tenses around me for a second then relaxes his muscles, allowing me deeper access.

I take advantage of his trust and slide my tongue inside him, working in and out while my hand finds his cock. I stroke him a few times but I know he's close so I shift his body down and reclaim him with my mouth.

My tongue resumes lapping down his length as my finger probes his now vacant hole. After one deep suck as far into my throat as he can go, Dylan pushes my hand so my finger is fully seated in him, finding his sweet spot as he erupts on my tongue. I can't keep it all contained so I swallow as much as I can while drops escape from the sides of my lips.

Dylan is like a statue as he clenches around my finger and rides out his orgasm in my mouth. After a few blissful moments, he gently pulls away and positions himself so he's lying on half of my body. "You look fucking hot with my come dribbling from your lips."

Instinctively, I lift my hand to wipe it but Dylan stops me.

"Let me," he whispers, leaning in for a soft kiss on each side of my mouth. With his juice on his lips, he kisses me, allowing me to share even more of his flavor as I lap it up.

Dylan's strong body curls around me, holding me while he slowly grazes every inch of my face with his swollen lips. Just as the heat is starting to intensify and our breathing is once again shallow, Dylan's phone rings on the night stand.

He freezes and pulls away. "Fuck." As soon as the phone is within inches of his face, Dylan barks into it. "What happened, Josh?"

Chapter Fourteen

Dylan

Motherfucker! This can't be happening. Not so soon after me taking charge here. I knew there would be people trying to challenge me for the position Sal just dropped in my lap. Plenty of people have been with the family much longer than me but I didn't think it would happen so quickly...whatever the hell *it* was.

"I've got to run downstairs." I'm stepping in my jeans as I quickly give Spencer some answers to the questions he's been whispering since my phone rang. "Josh has a situation with a couple of the guys and I need to check on things. I'll be back as soon as I can. Just make yourself comfortable."

I pull my shirt over my head and notice Spencer is also looking for his shirt. He looks to me with a serious expression. "I'll go with you."

How cute. I smirk and resist the urge to pat him on the head. "I don't think so. Just go to bed and I'll be here when you wake up."

"I might be able to help." He's getting dressed too. I actually chuckle.

"I appreciate that you want to but have you forgotten what business I'm in?" I toe into my sneakers and shove my heel in without unlacing them. Then I grab my Glock from my top drawer and slide it into my leg holster. "You don't need to be around that shit and I've got to focus."

"I won't distract you." He's fully dressed and ready to go. "I promise to just fade quietly into the background unless I can help with something."

His turquoise eyes are my undoing. I can't say no to him and maybe Josh is just being dramatic anyway? When he called, he said the three new guys all left their rooms at the same time, only twenty minutes after going in. And the guys they were with hadn't come out. As much as I want to believe it's all an innocent coincidence, I know something's up and I don't want Spencer around. But, I also like having him near me so I nod my head and we walk out the front door together.

The building is quiet. Most guests arrive between nine and midnight and are out by two so I'm not surprised to find the halls empty. What I don't like is the look on Josh's face when we exit the elevator on the third floor.

"What'd you find?" As soon as I hung up with him, Josh was heading into the apartments to make sure everything was okay. He was waiting outside of 312. Scott's apartment.

"Looks like they were drugged." Josh opens the door to the apartment and we follow him in. "Doesn't look like anything was damaged and they're all breathing fine."

"Who else?" I drop to my knees next to Scott's prone body. He's sprawled, fully dressed, in an uncomfortable looking position on the sofa but he seems to be sleeping peacefully. I brush back a few of his blond curls from his forehead and feel his temperature. He doesn't seem hot so I straighten out his legs and put a pillow under his neck. He's gonna hurt like hell in the morning.

"Travis and Georgie." Josh is already walking toward the door.

"Fuck! Georgie is still so green." I'm on Josh's heels as he walks two doors down to the next apartment. "Has any one called for an ambulance?"

Josh shakes his head as he opens the door for us. "Doc Jenner is on his way. He said if their vitals are good, we can let them sleep it off."

The front room is empty so I walk straight to the bedroom. This apartment isn't occupied full time but the layout is pretty much the same for all the one-bedrooms. I lived in one just like it when I first started working for Topher.

When I see Georgie, I feel my stomach drop. He's naked and tied to the four corners of the bed and his chest doesn't seem to be moving. "Fuck, Josh. You didn't untie him?"

I reach the bed in a few strides and hear Georgie snoring lightly. Thank god.

"I haven't been in here yet." Josh is at the other side, untying the scarf holding his wrist to the bed post. "I found Travis first, then Scott and was heading here when you walked up."

When I look back, I see Spencer is untying the scarf from Georgie's right ankle with a green hue to his face. He must be swallowing back the bile too. I shouldn't have let him come down with me.

I cup my hand around Georgie's cheek and feel that his temperature is normal. At least it feels normal to me. *Where the fuck is that doctor?*

"Was he..." Spencer's voice jolts me back into the moment. He nods towards his crotch and gives me a pained look. "You know..."

God, he better fuckin not have been hurt. I glance to Josh and he nods as I slide my hand under Georgie's right knee and pull it up and over so we can take a look at his back side. No blood or other mess to indicate he was penetrated at all.

The doorbell startles us as I drop his leg. I pull a corner of the sheet across Georgie's hips to cover him up a little while Josh rushes to the door.

Spencer seems to visibly relax once Georgie is covered.

Doctor Jenner has been a client for over twenty years and makes house calls whenever we need him. Topher didn't exactly offer medical insurance so Doc Jenner keeps the boys tested and vaccinated at reduced rates.

"He's in here." Josh's voice carries into the room before he and the doctor appear in the doorway. "He's the only one that was naked. The others were still dressed."

Doc Jenner nods politely to me and replaces me at Georgie's side. He's already got his stethoscope out and is counting heartbeats. He makes a few notes on his clipboard then pulls a blood pressure monitor from his bag. I don't realize I'm shaking until I feel Spencer's arm wrap around my shoulder.

"This isn't your fault," he whispers into my ear while the doctor writes more notes.

"It is." I shake my head but can't take my eyes off the sweet kid lying unconscious on the bed. "I'm supposed to keep him safe…all of them…and barely a week on the job and I've already let them down."

"You haven't let anyone down." He nudges me forward so I'm suddenly facing him. "You're taking care of them and doing the best you can. Do you know why someone would do this?"

"To get me out." I turn back to see the doctor pulling the comforter around Georgie and tucking it around him. "There are people that don't think I deserve this position. Truthfully, I don't. I don't know what the fuck Sal was thinking when he gave me the job…but I'm sure he'll be reconsidering it after tonight."

"Don't worry about that right now." He takes a step closer to the bed. "He looks like he's gonna be fine."

Georgie does look like he's sleeping off a bender. I catch the doctor's eye to get his opinion.

"Well, he looks fine. He's gonna have a bitch of a headache tomorrow but he should feel okay within a few days. Make sure he stays hydrated. Get him to drink water and go to the bathroom every time he wakes up but he'll be groggy for a day or two."

I nod and look to Josh. "We need to get him upstairs."

Josh leans forward to pick up Georgie when I raise my palm. "Leave him here for now. I want to see Travis."

We find Travis is a similar position to Scott. He's peacefully sleeping on the couch as if he dozed off during a movie. Doc Jenner gives us the same instructions for Travis and Scott as he did for Georgie. Lots of fluids and plenty of sleep. As soon as the doctor leaves, Josh calls two of the guys from his security team that weren't working tonight to play nurse to Travis and Scott. They can't be alone all day and I want to make sure they're protected if this isn't over.

From what we can tell, nothing has been stolen from any of the apartments and no one was actually injured.

"I don't get it. What's the motive?" I ask Josh once Bryce shows up to stay with Scott. I've heard they had a thing going but I didn't know it was true until he barreled through the front door and pounced on the bed next to Scott, crying into his neck like a lost child. We give them some privacy and retreat to the front room.

Josh is pacing by the window when Marco, his second in command, speaks up.

"We have video of them coming out of the rooms at the same time and stepping into the elevators. They went down to the garage but didn't exit the elevators."

"What do you mean they didn't exit?" I look from Marco to Josh, expecting a better explanation than that.

"We saw them leave and hit the button for the garage." Josh is still looking out the window as he's explaining. "At that point, we didn't suspect anything so we moved to other cameras. I don't usually watch people walk to their car, you know."

Okay, I guess that's fair. I nod and look back to Marco to continue.

"Per protocol, we expected the boys to check in within ten minutes. When none of them did, we started making calls."

"You've checked all the video footage?" I say to Marco.

He nods then takes a deep breath before slowly letting it out. I know whatever he has to say next isn't gonna be good.

"We have footage up until you get out of the elevator and meet with Josh, but everything shuts down at that point."

"What the fuck does that mean? How does everything shut down?"

Now I'm pacing and Josh is in Marco's face. "Explain."

"Well, the cameras all shut down. We did all the normal reboot procedures and Brad is tracing each line to see where the failure occurred but…"

"But what?" Josh and I say simultaneously.

"But, we don't have any footage for the past hour."

"Motherfucker! Why would they drug these guys but not rape or steal from them. It doesn't make sense. What benefit could you get from this?" I say to no one in particular.

"Distraction." Spencer's confident voice rings out. "That's what they got. What else is in this building that would be vulnerable if you two were stuck in here?"

Josh's phone rings right as I'm starting to piece things together.

"It's Bart," Josh says.

"Fuck. The art." I turn to the door and run out, opting for the stairs instead of waiting for the elevator. "Andre is up there."

Spencer and Josh are right behind me as I race up six flights to my penthouse apartment. The stairwell door requires a keycard to get through so I have to wait for Josh to catch up so he can let me in.

We enter the utility room and I barrel into the kitchen with my weapon drawn. The kitchen is clear so I look back to Spencer. "Stay here," I whisper before Josh and I slink into the front room.

At first glance, nothing is disturbed. But it's too quiet. Eerily quiet. I walk down the hall toward Andre's studio. As soon as we step through the doorway, I really panic.

"Andre." I'm turning toward his room when I hear an unfamiliar door creak open.

"In here." His squeaky voice stops me and I realize where it's coming from. I turn back to the guest bathroom and see the light flick on.

"Are you okay?" I hold Andre by the shoulders and give him a once over. "What happened?"

I can feel the tension leave his body as he collapses into my arms. His sobbing breaks my heart. I don't know what happened but it obviously shook him up enough to force him into hiding.

Spencer slowly approaches from behind and rests his palm on Andre's back. "You're okay now," he whispers.

His words remind me of the night I was shot and the way he kept me calm until help arrived.

He notices the open door inside the bathroom and peeks in. "Is that a panic room?"

I nod once and walk Andre back to his studio. The room is destroyed. All the forgeries are gone and paint is splashed across every square inch of floor and wall. It looks like a preschool class was left unattended with the finger paints.

I sit him on a stool as soon as his breathing is back to normal. "Can you tell us what happened?"

He nods and takes a shuddering breath before he starts.

"I was in here painting when I heard the elevators arrive. At first I thought it was Georgie but there were three voices and they weren't familiar. I went in the bathroom and watched to see what they were doing. They went straight into the studio. They had guns so I slipped into the panic room and watched on the cameras."

"What did you see?" I put my hand on his back to reassure him. "Who was it?"

Andre shrugs before continuing. "I don't know. I've never seen them before but they were looking for me."

"How do you know they wanted you?" I look around the room. "Looks like they just wanted the paintings and they got them."

"No." His voice cracks as he shakes his head and curls forward. "They wanted me. They took the paintings but they were looking into the cameras and telling me to come out."

I look at Josh. No one outside of our security team and closest friends know about the panic room exists much less where the cameras are that feed into it.

"Are you sure you haven't seen any of them before?"

"No, never." He looks up at me. "They said they'd be back for me. I think they want to continue with Topher's forgery business."

I pull him against my side. "They won't get near you. I promise."

"Can we watch the recordings from this room?" Spencer is back in business mode. He's been surprisingly quiet, just like he promised. Only interrupting when he has something to offer. So far he's two for two. I look to Josh.

"Those cameras are always running so they only save about sixty minutes back." He runs into the panic room and starts pulling out wires from hard drives. "Hopefully we haven't overwritten it all."

CHAPTER FIFTEEN

SPENCER

I don't know why I'm shocked when Dylan straps a handgun to his calf but I am. Although it wasn't nearly as shocking or terrifying as walking into that bedroom and seeing the sweet and flamboyant Georgie naked and tied to the bed. He didn't look like he was breathing at all.

But all of that still doesn't measure up to watching Andre tremble at the thought of strange men breaking into the apartment and trying to kidnap him...or worse.

There was only about twelve minutes of video that recorded the guys wrapping up the forgeries and walking out of the building with them. The two men we saw were well organized and knew how to avoid the cameras in the apartment, ensuring they were free to leave without detection once we were distracted on the third floor.

I can't help but wonder what would have happened if I stayed behind. I didn't know about the panic room so I would have been completely exposed to these intruders. Maybe they would have left me alone. Maybe they wouldn't have even known I was there. Or maybe they would have taken me instead. If ransom is what they're after, they would have been better off taking me.

It's the first time I genuinely question whether it's safe to be with Dylan. I want to be but his world doesn't fit well into my world. I come from the land of app moguls and advanced degrees and wine tastings. Guns and attempted kidnappings shouldn't be a part of my daily life but this is the second time in as many weeks that someone I know has been threatened by one while I'm just feet, or in this case floors, away.

"How you holdin' up?" Dylan sits on the sofa next to me and hands me a cup of coffee. "Do you take cream or sugar?"

I shake my head. "Black is good. Thanks."

The familiar flavor seems to center me. This is a crazy situation but it's not always like this. It can't be.

"How did they know where the cameras are?" I look to Dylan. He's tugging on the hair at the nape of my neck while staring out the window. The sun is rising but we didn't even try to go to sleep.

"Not many people know about them so it has to be someone on staff or someone close to Topher." He looks to the other sofa where Andre has passed out. Josh brought Georgie up and he's cuddled in his own bed. "Based on the fact that they only went for the paintings, I think they were close to Topher. Maybe he talked about partnering with them or something. He didn't tell me much."

"Are there other cameras in the apartment?"

He nods and looks into each corner. "Yeah, all the rooms…"

I can feel my eyes widening at the same time he realizes what he's said. "Please tell me we didn't make a sex tape tonight."

Dylan is tough and scary when he wants to be but he's terrible at holding back a smile. He purses his lips and tries to bite his cheeks but it doesn't work. He breaks out laughing. "God, I hope not." He buries his forehead against my neck. "That was definitely not my best work."

I throw my head back, cringing at the thought of a video circulating in my business circles of me giving a clumsy blowjob. "You're joking, right?"

He laughs even harder. "I wish I was." He takes a deep breath and places a light kiss on my jaw then rests his cheek on my shoulder. "I really do wish this was all a joke. I shouldn't have invited you back. You don't need this shit in your life. I'm really sorry about everything."

I know this isn't his fault and I'm being a pussy. He needs support right now, not one more person to worry about. It's time to put on my big boy pants and start coming up with solutions not more problems.

"Okay, fine. There's nothing we can do about that now." I shift in my seat so I can look into his eyes. "What do we do next?"

"*We* don't do anything." He's back in serious mode, acting like a bodyguard once again. "*You* will enjoy the rest of your weekend with Steve and Joey then head home and not think for another minute about this."

I'm about to open my mouth when he covers it with two fingers. "*I* am going to call Sal in a few hours and we'll deal with this from here. He may have a better idea of who's involved. If nothing else, I can get some of his boys to help with security for a while. We'll be good."

I tilt my head so Dylan's fingers fall in my mouth then close my teeth on them and shake my head. I swirl my tongue around them for a second before pulling away and letting them fall to my lap. "Uh uh. I'm already involved so I *will* be helping you and these guys stay safe."

Just then, Andre whimpers in his sleep then bolts upright. A sheen of sweat covers his face as his wide eyes scan the room. When he finds Dylan and I on the other side of the room, he leans back and starts to breathe again.

"Sorry. Did I scream?" Andre looks ashamed as he pulls the blanket up against his chest.

"No, not at all," Dylan says. He's so good with these kids. The perfect big brother. "You're safe."

Andre looks up toward me then back to Dylan. "Maybe I should leave? If they're after me, you and Georgie are just going to be in danger as long as I'm here."

"Absolutely not." Dylan walks to Andre and sits next to him. "You're not going anywhere."

"Maybe he's right." I feel both sets of horrified eyes land on me. "I mean, he could stay with me for a while until you figure out who's after him and why."

"With you?" Andre whispers. I can hear the uncertainty in his voice. I know mine hold the same quiver when I explain.

"I've got plenty of room so you can set up a studio." I look to Dylan. "You and Georgie are welcome to stay there too. No one will be looking for you there."

That's when I remember the cameras and look toward the corners Dylan indicated earlier. "Well, maybe they will now…"

"Shit." Dylan gets up and calls Josh. "Get these cameras out of here. Today. I want the whole apartment swept for bugs."

Dylan scrubs his hand over his spikey hair then holds the back of his neck. "I can't leave. I appreciate the offer but I've got to deal with this shit." He looks over to Andre. "You should consider Spencer's offer. You don't need to be here while we're figuring this out. I'll ask Georgie if he wants to go too. He's been itchin to get to Frisco so I'm sure he'll want to go."

Andre looks torn. I think he wants to come but I'm still a stranger and he has no reason to trust me. I get up and walk to him, slowly holding my hand out like you would with a strange dog. When he doesn't flinch, I rest my palm on his forearm that's wrapped around his knees.

"I promise you'll be safe there." I'm dying to ask if the haunted look on his face is solely from last night or the result of years another kind of abuse. But that will come in time. I hope he'll trust me enough someday. For now, I just want to offer him refuge. "You can even stay in the pool house if you want. You can have the entire place to yourself or you can stay in one of the guest rooms in the house. Whatever you're comfortable."

"Okay." The single word is barely a whisper but I feel better knowing Dylan can focus on finding the people responsible for breaking into his apartment and drugging his employees. And I'll sleep better knowing there aren't still people trying to get into Dylan's place.

Chapter Sixteen

Dylan

Georgie barely wakes up to puke a few times on Saturday and isn't fully awake until around noon on Sunday. He's conscious enough to tell us he doesn't remember a thing about Friday night and he doesn't want to go to San Francisco. I find myself almost begging him to go keep Andre company but he doesn't bite. He's got his eye on someone in the arcade and there's no changing his mind.

It's almost three in the afternoon and I'm helping Andre pack for an indefinite stay with my...friend. Bed buddy? Acquaintance?

"Are you sure this is okay?" Andre asks as he zips up a suitcase we found in Topher's closet.

"Of course." He's on the verge of tears so I reach out and pull him into my arms. "You know you don't have to go. It's totally your decision."

"I know." He sniffles and swipes at his eyes. Tears haven't quite fallen but are pooling. "I just don't want to put you and Georgie in more danger."

"I wish I could promise you'd be safe here but I can't do that." I sit on the bed and pull him down next to me. "The truth is, I know you'll be safer in California. At least for a little while until we figure out who's responsible for everything that happened."

"I don't even know Spencer. Why is he being so nice?"

I smile at this. "I think that's just the kind of man he is. He cares about you." I laugh. "He put his life on the line to take out Topher before he even met Joey, then he paid all my medical bills a few days after meeting me. It's just who he is."

"So, you don't mind?" Andre looks me straight in the eye.

"Why would I mind? I'll miss having you around but it's more important that you're safe than here."

"But since you guys are together, will it be weird?"

I've been asking myself the same question for the past day and a half. I don't love the idea but the truth is, Spencer isn't my boyfriend and we aren't exclusive so if he falls for Andre and they make a go of it, I'll just have to accept it. I'll never be happy about it but I can accept it.

"We're not actually together." Yet. Andre isn't stupid. He knows that's not entirely true but he nods and finishes packing.

~**~

It's been two hours since their plane landed in San Francisco and I haven't heard a word from Spencer or Andre. They both said they'd call when they got settled but they haven't. I've started and deleted five texts over the past twenty minutes but I'm trying to give them some space.

They're probably working out logistics like where the bathroom is, where Andre can set up a studio…where he'll be sleeping. Spencer mentioned a pool house. I hope Andre opts for the separate building but I know he won't. He won't want to sleep alone in a strange town when someone is after him.

Nope, he'll want to be as close to Spencer as possible. Probably on the same floor. Maybe even in connecting rooms. That way, if he has a nightmare, Spencer can calm him down. Would Spencer offer to sleep in his bed if he was afraid? Would he invite Spencer into his bed? Would Spencer sleep naked like he did with me or would he wear shorts?

The scenarios in my head are getting worse as the minutes tick by. My paranoia and jealousy is at an all-time high when two simultaneous texts come in.

Spencer's house is amazing. It's in the woods and has a view of the city. I can't wait to start painting.

Andre seems to be settling in well. We had sandwiches for dinner and I'm gonna work at home tomorrow to help him set up a studio. He should be fine.

I respond to Andre first.

Glad you're all set. Send me a picture of the view. Call anytime.

He must have already taken a picture because I barely send the text when a reply photo is waiting for me. It's hard to see much in the dark image but I can see enough dots of light to know it must be beautiful in person. I wonder if I'll ever be invited to see it myself.

After deleting a few messages that were coming out snarkier than I intended, I finally get a response out to Spencer.

I really appreciate your help. I know I can trust you with him.

There are a lot of ways for him to interpret that and I smirk to myself when I think about which route he'll go.

Well, I'm pretty sure I can keep him alive, if that's what you mean. Is it?

Do you think that's what I mean?

Okay, now I'm just messing with him. I can imagine the frustration he's feeling right now. Does he think I'm mad? Jealous? Joking?

I don't know. Can you call me?

It's getting late. We can talk tomorrow. I'm sure you're tired from your flight.

Please.

Even without those innocent aqua eyes staring me down, I still can't say no to the guy. I push the call button and he picks up immediately.

"Hey." I can tell by the clipped way he answers that he's nervous. I'm nervous too.

"You wanted me to call?" I'm playing dumb because I want him to say it first. I want him to make some kind of declaration or promise or something that will keep me from going insane while Andre is there.

"Well, yeah." I can hear him exhale slowly into the phone. "I couldn't tell if you were mad."

"Should I be mad?" I have to cover the mic so he doesn't hear me chuckle. He's too easy.

"No." There's a dull swooshing sound in the background. He must have stepped outside because the wind wasn't there when he first answered. "D-D-Dylan, you said this was okay. I th-th-thought you wanted him to come out here."

"I did." His stutter is adorable and I know that means I've made him suffer enough. Maybe he's not going to declare anything without a nudge. I swallow what I like to think of as pride but is really just stubbornness and let him off the hook. "I do want him there. I'm just…jealous, I guess."

"You're jealous?" His demeanor changes completely. "Of what?"

"I think Andre has a crush on you." That's the understatement of the fucking year. He doesn't let his eyes stray for more than five seconds when he's within twenty feet of Spencer. "And I don't like the idea of you guys hooking up."

"What?" Now he's laughing at me. "Are you serious? I'm almost ten years older than him. That would be gross."

I snort quietly and hope he doesn't hear. "Um, that would definitely not be gross, it'd be hot. And I'd be jealous. I mean, I know we aren't like…together or anything but—"

"We're not?" Spencer interrupts me. "What are we?"

"Oh." Excellent question and one I'm not sure how to answer. "Well, long distance relationships are hard and all but I don't like thinking of you with other guys."

Spencer is quiet for a minute and if it wasn't for the wind blowing across the phone, I would have thought he hung up. Finally, he says, "I don't really do casual sex. Um, I guess we should have talked about it before but I assumed we were exclusive...although when I say it out loud, I realize how stupid that—"

"Okay." It's my turn to interrupt him. I don't know why I say it but it's too late to take it back. Not that I want to.

"Okay, what?" He sounds hopeful but is still hedging.

"Okay, let's be exclusive."

"Are you just saying this because Andre is here? Because it's not like you aren't also living with a gorgeous kid that would love to be your full-time bottom."

"Spencer!" I laugh out loud. I'm usually the crude one. "Well, seeing Andre drooling over you might have spurred my jealous tendencies. But that's not the only reason."

"No? What other reason is there?" The wind dies down and I assume he's back inside.

"Are you gonna make me say it?" I can't remember ever feeling like a twelve-year-old girl the way I do with Spencer.

"I think I need you to." Now he's messing with me. "I might jump to the wrong conclusion."

"Because I like you and I want to see if there is something there before either of us screw it up by fucking around." I hope my frustrated huff doesn't sound like I'm pissed.

"Oh." Spencer clears his throat before responding. "Not too many ways to misinterpret that."

"So?" Now I'm starting to get pissed. If he doesn't feel the same way, it's better to know that sooner rather than later. Although before I sent Andre to be his bed buddy would have been even more preferable.

"Agreed." I can clearly hear the smile in his voice. I just wish I could also see the smile in his eyes. "I feel the same way…I just wanted to make sure we were on the same page."

"Good." It's getting late and I know I should let him go but I don't want to. "Well, I've got to get some stuff ready for the week."

"Yeah, me too." Spencer covers the phone and mumbles in the background. "And I should make sure Andre has everything he needs. I'll talk to you tomorrow."

"Okay, good night."

"Good night, Dylan."

Wrapping my arm around the pillow that still holds Spencer's clean scent on it, I fall asleep quickly. In the morning, I have to see Sal and I'm not looking forward to it.

Chapter Seventeen

Spencer

On Monday morning, I make a quick breakfast of oatmeal and blueberries then head into my study to work from home. I don't do it too often but truthfully there isn't anything I can do from my office that I can't do from home. I just like going in to ward off the loneliness of being single. It's ten thirty when Andre walks into the study.

"Hey, kid. I hope you slept okay."

"I did. Thanks." He steps in front of the large window and looks out into the wooded hillside. "It's almost too quiet out here." He arches his back and stretches his arms out wide in both directions.

"Yeah, I love it most of the time." I finish the email I'm writing and shut the lid to my laptop. "Whenever you're ready, we can head into town and pick up some art supplies. Maybe have lunch."

"Yeah, that sounds great." Andre walks around the four corners of the room. "The light is really great in here."

"You think?" I shrug and stare out the window at a barn swallow that's resting on a nearby tree branch. "I've never really noticed. I just like the view."

"It is beautiful. I'd love to paint it sometime."

"Of course." I stand and walk to him. "You're welcome to work in here anytime...whether I'm home or not. Consider the entire property your studio."

"Really?" His eyes are beaming as he looks at me. I didn't realize how close I stopped until he's within kissing distance. Oops.

"Really." I take a step back and pat his shoulder. "We can head out now if you want."

His cheeks pink up a little but he doesn't let the subtle rejection slow him down. "Yeah. I'll change and be ready in a few minutes."

Ten minutes later, we are on our way. Last night, I neglected to include the detached garage in my tour of the house so when we walk inside, Andre lets out a small gasp.

"You have a Model S?" He stops short as if afraid to get too close.

"Yeah, she's new." I feel a little embarrassed about the pretentious car but as an investor in Tesla, I wanted to support the company and the environment. And she really is a sweet ride.

Holding out the key, I step close enough for the door handles to pop out. "You wanna drive?"

This time his gasp is louder and he actually steps away from the electric car, shaking his head. "No way. I just got my license and haven't driven much. I'd probably crash it."

"I doubt that." I gesture to the other side so he can get in. "But you don't have to if you don't want to. You can take the FR-S anytime. I don't take that to work anymore because we have charging stations for the EV in my office garage."

"You'd let me drive this?" Andre runs his fingertips over the back of the red coupe. "I really haven't driven much. Topher sent me out on errands in his car now and then but not too often."

"Sure." I open the door to the Tesla and slide in. The engine starts before Andre is buckled in. Once I get off the property, I give him a taste of how well the car handles on the windy roads.

Curiosity gets the best of me and I can't help but pry a little bit. "So, why did you wait to get your license?"

His body shifts from relaxed to rigid with those words. I'm tempted to tell him he doesn't have to answer but I have a feeling he needs to talk to someone and maybe it'll be easier with me since I'm almost a stranger.

After a minute of awkward silence, he exhales and turns to me. "My dad was very controlling. He thought he could beat the sissy out of me. When that didn't work, he decided to not let me drive or play video games as an incentive to man up. He doesn't even know I got my license. My mom taught me how to drive while Dad was at work and she took me to get it but I wasn't allowed to ever drive his cars."

"Wow, I'm sorry. That must have sucked." No wonder the kid was so timid. "Well, I'll give you some driving lessons on the surface streets so you aren't stuck at the house all day."

His black eyes are unwavering as he nods. "That would be cool."

He has a genuine smile as he relaxes back into the seat. His hand goes to the thin chain around his neck.

"Is that from your mom?" I ask.

He tucks it into his shirt and fidgets with the seat belt across his chest. "No. My brother."

"Oh, you have a brother? I always wished I had one. Hell, I would have even been happy with a sister but I'm an only child."

"Mateo was great when I was little but once he realized I was gonna be a fruit, he started to distance himself. He's my dad's son all the way. My mom was decent to me but she couldn't go against the actual men in the house. She had to watch them treat me like shit until I could leave."

"When did you leave?" I pull into the University Art Store parking lot but don't take off my seatbelt.

"The day I turned eighteen." Andre's voice cracks but he keeps going. "My mom woke me up right after Dad left for work and said I needed to leave before my dad did something terrible. I didn't know what he had planned but I wasn't about to wait around to find out. I put some clothes in my backpack and walked out the door."

"Where did you go? Did you have any money?"

"My mom gave me forty bucks as I was leaving but she couldn't risk more than that. Dad counted every penny and would have known she helped me. I remembered Mateo talking about Topher running Paddles so I went there. I thought it was just an arcade. I didn't know about the other stuff."

I reach out and slide my arm across Andre's shoulder. "I'm glad you found a place to stay. Who knows what would have happened if you were just out on the streets."

He nods then leans his head back, resting it on my arm. "You have no idea how much I appreciate what you're doing."

"I'm happy to do it. You're like the little brother I never had." And with that, his smile falters and he looks away. Maybe Dylan was right about the crush.

I squeeze his shoulder to get his attention. "Ready to get some supplies so you can paint my backyard?"

"Yup." He opens the door and exits without a backward glance to me. He's either hurt or embarrassed and I don't want him to be either. But, it's better to set up some boundaries upfront so we can avoid an awkward encounter later.

The large store is overwhelming but Andre quickly zeros in on what he needs. He brought some paints and brushes but I know he didn't put much in his luggage. I grab a case of oils that look similar to what he had at Dylan's. "How about something like this?"

He glances at me and shakes his head. "Those are really expensive. I just need a few small tubes for now."

He's checking every price and only holding on to the most basic colors. "Don't worry about that. This is my welcome gift. Besides, I'm serious about wanting a picture of the yard."

"I don't want you to feel like you have to support me. I have some money."

That's a surprise. I got the impression he wasn't paid by Topher. "You do?"

His indignant smirk makes me smile. "Yes. Not much but Dylan paid me for the week I worked for him."

"Oh, good." I should have known Dylan would have given him some means of independence. "Regardless, I want you to select everything you need to paint me a few landscapes…and whatever else you want to paint for yourself."

"Are you sure? It'll be a few hundred bucks."

"Of course, Andre. Go crazy. I want you to be comfortable in my home for as long as you're there."

We left with almost a thousand dollars' worth of easels, canvases and paints. And Andre looked like a kid on Christmas morning.

"You must be starving. What are you in the mood for?"

"Anything is fine. I'm not picky."

"I am so how about Sushi, Thai or Italian?" Being an overindulged child meant I had a finicky palate.

"I like Sushi." Andre loaded the wider canvases in the back seat while I put everything else in the front cargo area.

"There's a great place down the street. We can walk."

~**~

As soon as we get back to the house, Andre sets up his easel and paints in the corner of my office. After a quick inspection of the other rooms, he deems my study as the best light so I go with it.

We move in a small table from the foyer so he has a place to work by the window and we settle into our projects. It's kind of fun to have someone in the room with me but I'm not really used to having anyone in my office so when my phone rings and I see my mom's name on the screen, I almost don't answer. When Andre nods toward the phone, asking if he should leave, I shake my head and answer the call.

"Hey, Mom."

"Hi, honey. How are you?" I can tell she's driving because the hands-free speakers echo in her Mercedes.

"I'm good. How are you?" I slide back from my desk and put my feet on it. These calls can be long if she's stuck in traffic.

"Busy as always. You know how I can't say no to anyone."

"I know. I hope you're at least having fun." I learned a long time ago not to play into her pleas for sympathy. She's the last person in the world that needs it.

"Fun is relative." She huffs and I can just imagine her inspecting herself in the rearview mirror to make sure she's perfect. Even in her fifties, she's just as high maintenance and fashion conscious as she was in her twenties. "I'm actually calling for a favor."

"What kind of favor?" My change in tone earns me a smirk from Andre. Even with his severely dysfunctional family, he obviously understands a mother's guilt.

"One of the major donors for the foundation is hosting an exhibit at Bach Gallery on Saturday and I need you there."

"Why do I need to be there? What kind of exhibit is it?"

"Well," she clears her throat and coughs twice, "it's actually themed around gay youth that are homeless."

"Oh." I can't help but look at Andre as she continues.

"It really is a shame that not all parents are as accepting as your father and I. I just don't understand it."

She's never been accepting of anything related to me being gay but I guess if the theme of the day is unconditional love, she's gonna roll with it among her socialite friends.

"I can probably do that." Andre laughs quietly and shakes his head at my easy acquiescence. *Oh yeah?*

"Mom, I have a friend staying with me. Can I bring him along?" Andre's eyes bulge and he shakes his head more seriously now. I can only give him an evil smirk as I nod. "He'd love to attend. He's been looking for a reason to put on a tux."

"A friend?" Her accepting attitude has suddenly changed. It's probably easier for her to love me unconditionally when I'm single. "Is he an intimate friend?"

"Mom!" We've never talked openly about guys and I don't really want to start. I know it's just ammo for her to use against me at some later date but since I brought it up, I have to give her something. "Andre is staying here for a while. The, uh, guy I've been seeing asked me to show him around the area."

"You have a boyfriend? Since when?"

I steal a glance at Andre and see his brush is hovering above the canvas but not touching it. I guess I'm saying this as much to him as Mom.

"He's not exactly my boyfriend but Dylan and I have been seeing each other for a few weeks." One week to be exact. Actually, a few days if our phone fuck was our first date. *God, was that our first date?*

"So you're not bringing Dylan?" Mom is clearly uncomfortable with the direction of the conversation but that's too bad. If she wants people to believe she's an accepting mother, I'm going to make her work for it.

"I don't know. He lives in Portland so I'll see if he can make it. Either way, Andre and I will be there."

I can already see Andre working on his excuse not to go but an art exhibit is the perfect place for him to meet some people and network.

When Mom finally says goodbye, I'm almost dreading the conversations I've got ahead of me.

CHAPTER EIGHTEEN

DYLAN

As much as I want to put it off, I can't avoid Sal any longer. As the current head of the DeMonaco family, the business is really his and if anything happens in it, he has to know. He's probably going to be pissed I waited two days to talk to him but I wanted to get some intel from Bart and Josh before I went crying to him.

Walking into Choppers in the middle of the day is always strange. The bike bar in the mountains is not the typical crime family headquarters but Sal is a weird dude. Instead of taking the helm of the business when his brother died, he let Topher step in and start some art forgery side business.

I know the guys are probably sick of seeing me but I try to act like I belong as I walk to the bar in the back and say hi to Bobby. "Can I get a beer?"

Bobby is the bartender but he's also one of Sal's closest confidantes. "Hey, Dylan. Back so soon?"

"I need to talk to the boss."

He hands me a frosty mug of beer and motions for me to follow. "Everything okay?"

I shake my head but don't say anything else until we're in Sal's office. Sal leans back in his chair and waits for me to sit at his long table desk. "How's the first week on the job?"

I feel like a complete failure but holding anything back could put lives in danger so I just lay it out on the line, explaining everything from the boys that were drugged to the break in and threats against Andre and following up with the fact that I sent Andre to go live with Spencer even though he and I have been hooking up. Both Bobby and Sal get a good laugh out of that.

"So, who do you think is behind this, Dylan?" Sal is eerily calm. I almost prefer the hulking man to be angry and loud.

"I don't know. Bart said the video feeds are new and only in the penthouse. It could be someone on the inside but not many people know about Andre."

"Who is not many?"

"Me, Georgie, Joey and Josh. I don't think Topher introduced him to anyone else and definitely not as an artist of any kind."

"You think it's someone on the outside?" Sal's calm is breaking a bit. He could easily take care of someone inside the family but outsiders could get messy.

225

I scrub my hand across my chin and lean back, looking up at the ceiling. "I hope it's an outsider because I trust every man working for me."

"Well, you'll learn soon enough who you can truly trust. For now, I'm sending a few guys over to meet with Josh and see what they can do to fortify the building." He nods to Bobby and the bartender slips quietly out the door behind us. "Those boys and the people in the arcade are your priority. Keep them safe inside the building and I'll see what I can find out on the outside. I have some contacts that might know who's targeting us and why."

I stand and extend my hand over the desk. "Thanks, Boss."

He shakes my hand and nods brusquely, dismissing me. Before the door closes, I hear Sal clear his throat so I glance back.

"You're doing good, kid. Just stay focused and you'll be fine."

I nod and walk down the hall, eager to be on my way.

~**~

I've been avoiding my sister for weeks so when I show up on her doorstep with takeout and a six pack, she jumps in my arms and gives me a wet kiss on the cheek. "Dyllie! I'm so glad you're here."

"Hey, Heather. Sorry I didn't call first." I glance around as I put the bag on her small dining table. "Where's my favorite niece?"

"Your only niece just fell asleep so be quiet in there."

I haven't seen Charlie Ann in almost a month and at ten months old, I know she's probably changed a lot. I peek into her crib and can't resist rubbing my thumb across her chubby hand. She's so beautiful.

I close the door quietly as I go back to the living room. "She's gorgeous, sis. I don't know where she gets it from."

"She takes after me. What can I say?" Heather has already spread out the Chinese takeout boxes across her coffee table and is sitting cross legged on the ground. I join her on the opposite side. "So why have you been avoiding me?"

"Busy." She doesn't know much about where I work and I plan to keep it that way. "I'm starting a new job as a manager so I'll be working longer hours but it'll be good experience."

"That's great, Dyl." She cracks open a fortune cookie then snorts. "I think this is meant for you."

As I open the crumpled strip of paper she tossed at me, she jumps up and runs to her fridge. "Oh, oh, oh. I've been meaning to tell you I want you to meet someone."

"Who?" Please let this be about a new guy in her life and not about me. Since her ex bailed as soon as she found out she was pregnant, I've been worried that she'll be alone forever. Much like I worry about myself.

"There's a guy that moved in upstairs that would be perfect for you. Here's his card."

The card she shoves in my hand is for a massage therapist named Patton Oliver. "Uh, thanks. A massage would actually feel pretty good right now."

"Well, he can give you a 'special massagie' with a happy ending if you play your cards right." Her fake Chinese accent is comical and a little offensive to all Asians but I have to laugh.

"Is that right?"

"Definitely!" She sits back in front of her food and shovels some beef and broccoli in her mouth. "He's gorgeous and single and he just moved here so he doesn't know a lot of people. I tried to woo him with my feminine wiles but he swings your way so I figured if I can't have him, at least I could look at him for the rest of my life."

"Thanks." I slide the card in my back pocket with no intention of ever calling him.

"I'm being serious, Dyl. You need a man. You seem lonely."

I cock my head and stare her down. "I'm the one that needs a man?"

"I'm too busy for a man right now. Charlie is enough. You, on the other hand, have been pouting lately so you should at least schedule a massage and get to know him."

I shove an egg roll in my mouth and look away.

"Dylan, please. I can call him right now and have him come by for a beer." She reaches for her phone on the sofa but I grab it first.

"I'm seeing someone." I wasn't going to mention Spencer but she didn't leave me much choice.

"You are? You swear? Who is he? How did you meet? Do you have a picture?"

Damn, I need a picture. I should have taken one before he left. I make a mental note to ask Georgie if he has one. He's the queen of sneaking photos when people aren't looking. He's the queen of a lot of things.

"Yes, I swear. His name is Spencer and it's still pretty new but I like him."

"When can I meet him? I can get a sitter for Friday and we can go to dinner."

I hold out my hands to signal for her to slow down. She's always been a mile-a-minute kind of girl and it can be overwhelming. "He lives in Cali so I don't know when you'll be able to meet him but maybe in the next few weeks. I'll find out his schedule."

Her excitement is quickly contained. "Oh. It's long distance?"

She knows first-hand how difficult a remote relationship can be so I'm not surprised when she reaches for her phone. "Let me just call Patton and see if he can come by for a little while."

Anxious to get her off my back, I let her make the call and am relieved when she reaches his voicemail and has to leave a message.

"Thanks, sweetie, but I'm fine. Spencer is cool and we'll see what happens."

She isn't completely buying it but she lets it go. "So how did you meet this Spencer?"

Oh. Right. "He was looking at an apartment downtown and we met through a mutual friend." That's mostly true.

"Oh, he's moving here? Awesome. Let me know when we can all get together so I can get a sitter."

"Yeah, sure."

After placating her, we move onto more neutral topics like where she should go for new tires and if I like the purple stripe in her hair.

~**~

By the time I finally get home, Georgie is working and I'm alone in the apartment. I can't remember the last time I was truly alone there and it's a little depressing. I want to call Spencer but I don't want to seem needy.

After a quick shower, I crawl into bed and pass out, not letting myself wonder too much about the men that surrounded me just a few days earlier and where they are while I lay alone.

Chapter Nineteen

Spencer

I don't think he realized it, but on Monday, Andre didn't leave my side for more than five minutes all day. Like a second shadow, he was always there. Surprisingly, it didn't bother me as much as I would have expected it to.

As I head in from my morning run on Tuesday, he's sitting in the kitchen with a cup of coffee.

"Good morning." I pat his shoulder as I pass behind him. "You're up early."

"Yeah." He has both hands cradling the mug and doesn't look up as he takes a sip.

"Everything okay?" I slide into the chair next to him and wait for him to make eye contact. When he finally does, he just nods.

"Andre, what's going on?"

"Sorry." He shrugs and looks out the window again. "I think I'm just nervous about being alone here."

"Oh, hey." I scoot closer and wrap my arm around his back, not worried about the fact that I'm damp with sweat and probably smell terrible. "You'll be fine. I have a super high tech security system and no one knows you're here."

"Do you have cameras in the house?" His eyes bounce to the corners of the room.

"Not inside but there is a full surveillance system surrounding the property. The previous owners liked their privacy." I can tell he's not reassured. "Would you feel more comfortable if I did have cameras inside? I can probably get someone out here tonight to do it if you'd like. I'm on the board of a company that offers smart home electronics and the cameras are really easy to install."

"I don't want you to completely change the way you live just because I'm being a baby." He straightens up in my arm and leans forward. "I'll be fine."

I let go and scoot around to the side of the table so I can see his face. "Would you like to come to the office with me? You can paint the city scape or help out Barbara and Elliott. They always complain about needing another pair of hands for scanning mail and data entry."

"Really? I'd love to." He jumps up. "I can be ready in a few minutes. Wait, what should I wear?"

"It's casual. Jeans and a t-shirt are fine."

~**~

As expected, Barbara immediately puts Andre to work on a stack of invoices that need to be scanned into the accounting system and Elliott drags him to lunch with the girls. No one has asked but I think they think he's related to me so they're all on their best behavior. I can't wait to get the scoop from him about what they all had to say.

After having most of my dates for the past few years end up on tech rag sites and even in a few newspapers, I've avoided dating. I've also kept my social life completely separate from business. That was always easy because I don't have much of a social life but now that I have a live in boy toy that I'm bringing to the office, rumors are going to fly.

While Andre is out, I send a quick note to Dylan.

Hey, Dylan. Busy?

Not really. Going over some of the books. How are things there?

Great. Andre spent yesterday painting and came into the office with me today. He's the shiny new toy that my receptionist is showing off around town.

While I'm waiting for his response, I make an appointment with my personal shopper at Nordstrom. Andre will need a suit for Saturday.

Is he okay with that? He's pretty shy.

So far so good. I'm even taking him to a gallery event on Saturday. Any chance you want to come down here and join us?

What kind of event?

I'm surprised he's considering it but I shouldn't be. Dylan knows art better than I do. He picked some beautiful forgeries when I was pretending to be a buyer.

It's a charity thing my mom is organizing. She actually wants to show me off as the gay son that she 'loves anyway.'

That sounds tempting but not sure about meeting the parents yet. But thanks for asking.

Ouch. I shouldn't be hurt by his response but I am. When he said he wanted to see where we could take this relationship, I thought he was serious. Apparently, he still needs time.

Okay. I should get back to work. Have a nice day.

You too.

~**~

When Elliott corners me, I know exactly what's coming. This guy falls in love every weekend and is heartbroken by Friday night when it's time to go out and start over again.

"Please, please tell me you aren't into Andre." Elliott's palms are pressed together as if he's praying to me.

"I'm seeing someone so no, there's nothing going on with me and Andre." I lean against the corner of the wall and cross my arms. "Why? Are you interested?"

"Hell yeah!" Elliott hops on his toes like he's got to take a piss. "He's like your mini me. I love him."

Fuck. Here we go. "Elliott, he just got into town and I'm not sure if he's ready to roll with your crowd. Maybe give him a little time to get acclimated before you start planning the wedding."

"I know I say this all the time but I really mean it." He's holding both my wrists as he pleads with me. "You have to believe me when I say he's perfect. Exactly what I'm looking for."

"I have heard that before." I smirk and take a step back. "Many, many times."

"Just watch, Spence. He'll love me too."

"Whatever you say."

I want to warn Andre about the tornado that is Elliott but when I see him step into the hall and notice Elliott at the other end, he turns and heads back the way he came. Andre is a smart kid that probably has Elliott all figured out.

On the drive home, Andre is quiet so I have to ask. "So, what did you think of everyone?"

"Barbara is really nice. She seemed happy for the help."

"She loved having you there. She even asked if we could hire you full time." Andre's head spins around and his gaze locks with mine. "She did?"

"Of course. You did half her work today." I laugh and lightly punch him on the thigh. "You're her new favorite person."

He's beaming at the praise so I let him bask in it for a minute. "She's not the only person who's smitten with you."

"Ugh, please don't remind me." He throws his head back on the headrest and grabs the seatbelt at his chest. "Is Elliott like that with everyone?"

"Not everyone but he does have a lot of boyfriends."

"He kinda reminds me of Georgie but way more intense. Georgie just wants to flirt and maybe hook up. Elliott seems ready to pick out china."

"He falls hard and fast but then he moves on even faster."

"God, I hope so!" Andre is adorable when he's frustrated.

"Give him a week and he'll back off. By this time next week, he'll have a new soul mate and you can just be one of his many besties."

"Let's hope." He's fidgeting with the chain around his neck when he speaks again. "So what did you tell Barbara?"

"About what?" Traffic sucks and I've already forgotten what we were talking about while trying to avoid motorcycles and semi-trucks.

"When she asked if you could hire me," he whispered.

"Are you interested?" I steal a glance in his direction. Andre's big eyes are almost glowing.

"Yeah, of course. I need a job and I like working with you."

I smile and nod. "I like working with you too. You're welcome to come on board. I can pay you as a temp for now so you can see if you like it. I was thinking you might want to do something a little more artistic."

"Meh. Unless you want me to start forging again, it's pretty hard to make money in art. I wouldn't even know where to begin and I'm not sure I'm talented enough to bother. I need to be realistic about my long term job opportunities."

"That's a very pragmatic approach." I'm proud of the kid. It's actually the speech I've wanted to give him for a few days but I didn't have the heart to dish out one more disappointing reality. He's had enough of those.

"So I've got the job?" His quiet voice is shaky.

"It's yours if you want it." I hold out my hand for him to shake between our two seats.

Andre grabs it with more strength and confidence than I've seen from him yet. "Thanks, Spencer. I won't let you down."

By the time I arrive home, a network attack has the entire company on red alert. This isn't the first time we've been targeted by hackers but it's the first time they've gotten close enough to require that we take the servers completely offline. All my best programmers are working around the clock to get the security breach closed and ensure nothing critical was compromised or customer data accessed.

I'm like the walking dead on Thursday morning when I get a call from Dylan.

"Are you guys okay?" His voice is frantic and desperate, more so than I'd expect from such a strong man.

"We're fine. Are you okay?" I know he's not and that makes me nervous. I haven't seen Andre yet so I start walking toward his room as I wait for Dylan to respond.

"I think they struck again." Now I hear more than desperation. He's in actual pain. I stop walking and lean into the wall.

"Dylan, what happened? Are you hurt?" As I'm standing there, Andre walks out of his room and rushes to my side.

"What's wrong?" Andre leans toward the phone to hear the other side of the conversation but Dylan isn't speaking.

I hit the speaker button and almost shout. "Dylan, what's wrong. Tell me what happened."

"My sister." His voice cracks and he's almost whispering. "There was a fire at her apartment. My little niece."

"Dylan, are they okay? Is the baby okay?" I grab Andre's wrist and we start walking to the garage.

"They'll be okay." I know he's struggling to hold himself together. "But it was so close. They were sleeping. The neighbors said something was blocking the front door when they tried to bust in. They had to break a window and wake up Heather. She almost didn't wake up, Spencer."

I stop walking and sit on the porch steps. I know my eyes are welling up just out of empathy for Dylan. "Shh, Dylan. It's okay, babe. They're going to be okay. Are they at the hospital?"

The scratching on the phone makes me think he's nodding his head. I would give anything to be with him right now. He needs comfort and he's all alone.

"They didn't have to go to the hospital. Charlie's bedroom door was closed so she didn't have as much smoke exposure. Heather needed oxygen for about an hour but she refused to go to the hospital. They're both here with me."

"Do you want us to come? We can be on a plane within the hour."

"I knew you'd say that." His voice is steady now. "You're such a good person."

"We'll be there by noon. Just stay with your sister and wait for us."

"No, wait." He exhales into the phone and there's silence for a few seconds before he speaks again. "I'm okay. I just needed to talk. I still think you guys are safer there. I'll let you know what we find out but don't come yet. I don't want to have to be worrying about all of you."

"Dylan, you shouldn't be alone. You need company."

"Georgie's here. He's actually really good with babies and Heather has been able to get some rest. I'll let you know if I need you. I promise."

"Okay." I want so badly to be there but I know he's right and he needs to focus on his family. "I'll call in a few hours to check on things."

"Thanks, Spence."

"Talk to you later."

~**~

The shit storm at work didn't end until late Friday night. By the time we were able to isolate the corrupt servers and get a new data center online, I'd had to smile and assuage the minds of investors, customers and partners more times than I can count.

Dylan checked in often with reports about his sister and niece and they had additional security at Paddles which included a restriction on new clients. I worried about his well-being but was confident he knew how to take care of himself.

I climb in bed by nine pm on Friday and don't move until I hear pounding on the door at eight o'clock Saturday morning.

The pillow is over my head when I feel something land across my back. "Wake your lazy ass up, Spence. We need you today."

Greg is one of my closest friends from college. I sub on his softball team when they are down a player but I'm in no shape to play today. "Sorry, man. I can't."

"Why not?" He pulls back the blankets. I'm thankful that I didn't step out of my boxers when I passed out last night. Since Andre's been in the house, I've been careful to stay dressed as often as possible. "You don't look maimed or incapacitated. You look ready to play softball."

"Dude, I've had the week from hell. I'm not playing today."

He flops on the bed next to me. "Did that kid that let me in keep you up all night?"

So that's how he made it past my security system. "No, a bunch of shit went wrong at work." I groan at the thought of what I still have to deal with for the coming weeks. Maybe months.

"You mean that hacker thing? God, you're such a drama queen. Do you gay guys actually get periods too?"

I give him a light kidney punch and try to pull my blanket back up. "I've hardly slept all week. I'll be useless on the field."

"You're always useless. We just need a human to put on the shirt and ride the bench. You can sleep on it for all I care." He's poking my arm to annoy me into consciousness. Sadly, it's working. "Oh, does the boy toy play? We could use him too."

"I doubt he wants to spend his Saturday having a ball thrown at him by a bunch of strangers."

"Where is he? I'll ask him while you get dressed."

"He's probably painting in my office. But don't force him if he says no."

"Me? No means no. That's what my mama taught me." He smacks my ass as he jumps from my bed. "Now get your sorry ass up and meet me downstairs in ten minutes or you're gonna regret it."

"I hate you." I scream as he bounds down the stairs.

"Love you too." Greg is laughing all the way to my office.

That asshole is lucky he's so good looking or I would've stopped hanging out with him years ago. He's too damn perky in the mornings.

With a lot of grumbling and caffeine, Andre and I both manage to have fun playing softball. We were each only at bat twice so the pressure was relatively low and the exertion required to get through the game wasn't unbearable. By the time we have lunch and a beer with the rest of the team, it's four o'clock and we need to start thinking about that stupid gallery dinner thing for my mom.

I would have bailed all together but Rayna Bach is known for taking aspiring artists under her wing and giving them exhibitions when no one else will. I really want her to meet Andre. If they hit it off, maybe I'll invite her up to the house to see his work.

So, with tailored tuxedos and my check book in hand, we leave the house at six thirty to meet up with my mom and her rich cronies.

Chapter Twenty

Dylan

I've never known fear like when I got a call from a detective to tell me my sister's apartment was involved in a fire. I'm fairly sure my heart stopped beating until he explained that she and her daughter were okay but needed a place to stay.

Heather and I have always been close but since my mom died, we've drifted from my dad. His drinking got worse and it's difficult to be around him at all these days. He's only met his granddaughter once and that was on Father's

Day. Who knows if he'll even make it to next Father's Day.

When I see Heather sitting in the back of an ambulance with my sleeping niece in her arms, I'm ready to commit my eternal devotion to a god I've never believed in just for sparing their lives. They are my only family and I couldn't go on if something happens to either of those girls.

"We're okay, Dyllie." She nods in the direction of a group of neighbors. "Patton saved us."

"Patton?" My mind is still focused on inspecting them for injuries. Other than some soot smudges on their clothes, both angels in my arms seem fine.

"My hot neighbor." She looks over at him. "Oh, he's coming over here. Look sexy."

I roll my eyes and try my best to wipe away any traces of tears. By the time he's standing over me,

I can see why Heather was so excited for me to meet him.

Patton looks about my age but he's a few inches taller and has the long blond hair of a surfer. His eyes are dark, which seems unusual for his light hair but his tanned skin confirms a life of sunshine.

"You must be Dylan?" He extends his hand as I'm still gawking at his chiseled jaw and hugely bright smile. "I've heard a lot about you."

I take his hand and smile back. "Sorry about that. My sister can be a little overzealous sometimes."

He laughs an easy going chuckle that helps put me a little bit at ease. "Well, I don't think she was too far off but it's nice to meet you, despite the circumstances."

His grip is firm and I remember his card. You wouldn't know he makes his living with his hands by how silky soft they are. All that oil must keep his skin moist. I return his shake and take a step back.

"Hey, thanks for saving my girls here." I sit next to Heather on the edge of the van. "I really owe you. Anything you need, just ask."

His eyes twinkle as he gives me a quick once over. "It was nothing. You don't owe me anything."

I don't know how to read him but I know I need to say goodbye to him. "Well, it was great meeting you. I need to get them to my place so we'll see you around. Thanks again."

He smiles at me then leans into Heather for a quick side hug. He seems like a genuinely good guy. It's not the first time I've met a guy I wish was straight and interested in my sister. She deserves a man like him. Her and Charlie both.

~**~

As much as I told Spencer and Andre should stay in California, I keep waiting for them to walk through my door. I've made a point of texting Spencer and Andre a few times each day since the fire to give them another opportunity to insist on coming but after the hack attack at his company, I know Spencer needs to focus on work so I keep telling them I'm fine and will see them soon.

Heather went back to work today and Georgie actually offered to babysit so we're taking turns with diapers and books to keep Charlie entertained. It's not until Heather walks through the door at four thirty on Saturday afternoon that I make the decision to head to California.

I want to surprise Spencer so I don't tell him I'm coming. I just pack a few things and drive straight to the airport, leaving my sister and niece under the watchful eye of my security team.

It's almost nine when I pull the rental car into the wooded lot that Spencer gave me as his address.

I drive around the large home and park off to the side and out of the immediate view of arriving cars. I want him to be surprised when he finally sees me. And a small part of me is trying to catch of glimpse of him and Andre as they get home. See just how close they've become over the past week alone together.

With my car stowed in a dark corner of the property, I walk back toward the pool and settle in one of the cushioned loungers. I know they are still at the gallery so I kick off my shoes and lean back, resting my eyes for just a minute.

I'm not sure how long I've been out but low voices and a splashing sound wakes me up. A bit disoriented, I glance around the pool to see if someone has joined me but I'm still alone. Remembering my plan to surprise Spencer, I get up and quietly walk back toward the front of the house. It takes my eyes a minute to adjust but when I see two dark figures standing near the garage, I step back into the shadows to watch.

At first, the two people are just talking but when one turns and walks toward the main house, I realize he's carrying a gas can. The can is tilted so a trail drips across the lawn as he walks but when he passes a dim garden light, I recognize his face immediately.

Ivan was one of Topher's long term lovers. They'd been spending more time together but I didn't realize they were serious. Topher made it clear that he'd never settle for just one man so to see Ivan at Spencer's house and obviously trying to destroy it is a shock.

I'm trying to piece together whether or not Ivan knows anything about Andre and the paintings when my jaw drops and I let out a gasp. The second man steps into the light and I recognize Travis, one of the guys that was drugged with Scott and Georgie. I can't believe he's in on it. I feel betrayed and stupid for not realizing it sooner. He was overly interested in how the investigation was going and I thought it was just for his own peace of mind. It never occurred to me that he was our mole.

Having heard my shocked breath, they both look in my direction but I'm still hidden. I take a careful step back and pull out my phone. I've just thumbed out a text to Sal to tell him who's involved when I hear a loud whoosh and the dark night is glowing red.

They've set the garage ablaze and are now looking for me. The ground is dark and full of dead leaves so walking quietly into the woods isn't easy. Just as I turn toward my car, I'm face to face with Travis.

"What are you doing here?" I ask, trying to appeal to his conscience. "If this is about money, we can take care of that. Don't go down like this." I slowly reach for his forearm but he jumps back.

"This is your fucking fault, Dylan." His eyes are wild and dilated. He's clearly not himself. "You should have minded your own damn business. Topher would have taken care of you forever. All of us."

I'm not sure what he's talking about but when I sense Ivan behind me, I twist around and kick him in the gut before lunging at Travis. He's surprised by my sudden attack but not for long. Travis and Ivan both dig in their coats for weapons while I try to take down the larger of the two.

Travis is built tall and wide but he's not very smart. He's expecting me to punch high so I knee him in the balls and twist his neck, not intending to do serious harm but when I hear his neck crack and feel his body go limp, I know he's gone.

In the seconds it takes me to realize what I've done, I feel the hard barrel of a revolver dig into the small of my back. Even through the light shirt

I'm wearing, I know the cold metal is vibrating with the anticipation of Ivan pulling the trigger. I freeze and release my grip on Travis's lifeless body.

"I can help you, Ivan." I just need to keep him distracted long enough to get the upper hand. "I can get you want you want."

"Pick up that idiot and carry him inside."

Without looking back, I lift Travis into my arms and step forward when Ivan nudges me with the barrel. "Where do you want me to take him?"

"The garage. I needed an extra body anyway." He chuckles low. "Now I've got two. This is even better than I planned."

I can hear the shattering of glass from the garage as I approach the burning building. The fire hasn't spread to the main house yet but the garage is fully engulfed.

"Get him inside."

As soon as I'm within ten feet of the building, a wall of heat stops me as if it were made of bricks. "I can't get any closer. It's too hot."

"You're a strong guy." He presses deeper into my spinal column. The sensation almost makes me lose my footing as I arch away from him. "Toss him through the window if you have to."

Quickly surveying the building, I realize the back window has smoke pouring out of it but no flames yet. With a bit of a jogging start and a full swing of Travis's body around mine, I let go and toss him into the open window. He lands halfway in before his body gets caught by the jagged glass. At least he went in feet first so it looks like he was trying to climb out when he succumbed to the smoke and heat.

"You should be closer to the main house so I don't have to carry your ass up there later." Ivan yanks my arm toward the house. "Move it. Get on the back porch."

I can hear crunching sounds and the distant wail of a siren but by the time any kind of help arrives, I'll be another casualty of this house fire and Spencer and Andre will still be at risk.

With each step I take, I'm silently praying Sal got my message and will know who to hunt down. Maybe he'll find Ivan before Ivan finds Spencer and Andre.

The sirens are getting closer but not close enough. Ivan drops a match against the side of the house and the lower wall quickly ignites. It'll just be a matter of minutes before the whole house is a raging inferno.

"Check the back door." I climb the three steps to the door and turn the knob. Surprisingly, it's unlocked. I push gently and open it.

As I'm about to step into Spencer's home for the first and last time, I hear the crunch of bone then the barrel slides away from me.

I turn around. Spencer's standing over Ivan's body with a baseball bat. I'm in complete shock. Ivan is unconscious but still holding the gun so I kick it out of his hand and step toward Spencer.

"How did you do that?"

"I left my car on the street when I saw the flames. Andre told me to take one of the bats from my car. I never expected to find you here. Or him."

I can't help the grin as I pull him into me. "We need to call the police."

"They're here. They came behind the fire truck." It's only then I realize two large trucks are in Spencer's yard and more emergency vehicles are following. "Pull him off the porch. We need to get away from the house."

Half dragging, half carrying, we dump Ivan's body at the far end of Spencer's driveway while the hoses begin to water both burning buildings.

Andre appears at my side and pulls me into his slight frame. His body is convulsing with sobs as I rub his back and reassure him that I'm alright. Andre is in my arms but my eyes don't leave Spencer's as I quickly tell them what I've learned and how Travis was involved.

"Does this mean it's over?" Andre pulls back to look at me then at Spencer. "Are we safe now?"

I rest my head on his shoulder as I pull Spencer into us. "I hope so. They didn't mention anyone else so I hope this nightmare is over."

Chapter Twenty-One

Spencer

By Halloween, the crisis with our system attack was old news. The rev release is on track and the acquisition is a go. Andre capitalized on the opportunity to network at my mom's gallery event and was invited by Rayna Bach to work as her apprentice while she prepares for one of the biggest spring showcase events of her career.

"You're coming up on Friday, right?" Steve asks on the phone while I'm driving home from work on Wednesday evening.

"Yeah. Dylan is insisting I wear a costume. I think I'm coming as a computer geek." The last costume I wore was a toga in college and I'm not doing that in a room full of sexy prostitutes or anyone else for that matter.

"He's going to be Lex Luther. I think he wants you to be Superman." Steve chuckles lightly as I groan. If only that was a joke.

"I know. He's mentioned it a few times." I'll probably do it just to make him happy but I won't like it. "I'd be a much better Clark Kent."

"Nah, you're the perfect Superman." His voice takes on a serious tone after he clears his throat. "You've saved the day a few times and you should be proud of your new hero status."

Ha! I'm definitely no hero. I might have knocked out a guy but it wasn't beyond what anyone else would have done. The local sheriff has been quick to boast his own local hero that helped stop a man accused of several murders along the West Coast and leading a drug ring in the Pacific Northwest. I just try not to think about it too much. I've been much more interested in Dylan and his job.

"What are you and Joey wearing?" Now it's Steve's turn to groan.

"That kid has a thing for Sons of Anarchy so we're going as bikers."

"Yeah? That's not so bad." Steve has always been a biker at heart and only recently gave up his leathers for what he considers to be more business casual attire. "You'll both look great."

"I know." I can almost hear his smirk. "We always do."

"Yeah, yeah." He's a cocky son of a bitch. "I gotta go. I'll see you Friday."

~**~

When Friday rolls around, I leave work early to take the four o'clock to Portland. I don't bother packing a costume because I know Dylan has one waiting for me.

When I open the door to his penthouse, Dylan pulls me into his bare chest before I can even drop my bag.

"God, I've missed you." He can barely speak between kisses along my mouth and jaw. His hands are pulling on my belt buckle as he drags me into the bedroom. "I need you so fucking bad."

"Um hmm." I haven't seen him in three weeks and we still haven't been able to fully consummate the relationship. Every time we've been together, we've been dealing with one tragedy or another so this weekend is just for us.

He's planned a costume party on the second floor and then we'll spend the rest of the weekend in bed. He's made a lot of promises during phone sex that I expect him to make good on.

We don't have time for more than a quick sixty nine to release the tension but I'm counting down the minutes until we can ditch the party and I really show him how I'll be his Superman.

Georgie arrives as Katy Perry and is the second most beautiful girl in the room. Of course, Dylan's sister Heather is just as tan as he is but she carries herself in such an easy going manner that she and Georgie are inseparable for the whole night.

The catered appetizers are delicious and I let myself have a few more drinks than usual but all I can think about is getting Dylan back into his room. He's working the crowd and introducing me to people now and then but I've never been great at parties. I'm more of an observer and the people watching is better than I've experienced in a long time. While holding up a wall in the darkest corner of the room, Steve sidles up to me.

"Having fun yet?"

"Yeah. But I'm anxious to get out of here." I wiggle my eyebrows and he doubles over laughing.

"God, you're a dork. How have you ever managed to get laid with those kind of moves?"

I smack his arm. It's covered in tattoos and bulges out from the leather vest he's wearing. The assless chaps were a bit much but he loves the attention. And more than that, I think he loves the shades of red Joey sports every time they catch each other's eye. Steve has always been big on the shock factor.

"Things good with you and Joey?" I know the answer but I like to hear him say it.

"He's amazing." He leans against the wall next to me. "I don't know when he's gonna wake up and realize he's too good for me but I'm loving it. And him."

I look up and hold his eye. "Yeah?"

"Yeah." He takes a drink and stares at his young lover. "I've never been happier."

I give him a half hug, careful to keep my arm well above his bare cheeks. "I'm so happy for you. Both of you."

"Thanks, Spence. And what about you?" He laughs and seeks out Dylan in the crowd. "Dylan's been a wreck without you around."

"Really?" My faint smile grows a bit at this revelation.

"Like you don't know that." He snorts. "He comes by all the time and always manages to ask about you and what you've said about him and what you're planning to do after you sell Styleopia."

My grin now spreads into an obnoxious display of my years of whitening and braces. "Well, I haven't made any decisions yet but I do hope he's a part of them."

As if on cue, Dylan is beside me. "You almost ready to get out of here?"

I nod eagerly. Words aren't necessary when he can read my body language so well. I need him!

"Let's go." Dylan's voice is low and hungry. Just as needy as mine.

We work our way quickly through the crowd, nodding and saying good night to people as we move. All eyes are on us as we exit the banquet hall.

"You look hot in that leotard." I look down at the ridiculous costume he made me wear.

"Well, get a good look because you're never gonna see me in it again." I press Dylan up against the back of the elevator as we wait for our floor. I kiss him hard and rub my hand over his almost bald head. "And you look pretty good as Lex. I just hope you're feeling bendy."

Dylan grinds his cock into mine. In the stupid unitard, my dick is standing at full attention with nothing to hold it back. "I'll bend any way you want, baby." His palm rubs against my dick before he grabs a hold of it. "And then I'm gonna bend you just the same."

We are nearly naked by the time we make it to the room. Andre stayed in California to attend a Halloween party with Elliott and Georgie told us not to wait up so we can make as much noise as we want.

We don't waste any time before Dylan has me spread open on the bed. His mouth is on mine while his hands explore the skin he hasn't touched in weeks. I throw my head back as his tongue traces each of my pecs then stops at my right nipple. He sucks and nibbles the small points, causing me to buck into him. "Fuck, that feels good, Dylan."

"You taste good, baby." He moves to my left side and repeats the torture to my pebbled skin. "So good."

I can't stand it anymore. "I want to be inside you, Dylan."

"Yes." He kneels over me and reaches for the supplies in his nightstand. "Do it. Fuck me."

As much as I want this to be slow and gentle, neither of us are capable of gentle right now. The tension of the past month has kept us too wound up. First we fuck. Then we'll try gentle.

Dylan is hovering over me when I pull his neck down and kiss him hard, violating his mouth as my finger violates his hole. I'm trying to be easy when he flips me over so I'm on top of him.

"I'm ready, baby." I don't make him beg. Without taking my eyes off Dylan's, I push into him in one quick thrust. He presses against me as I pull both of his legs up to my shoulders. With him almost bent in half, I pound into him, reveling in the way his tight channel fits my shaft like a glove. I press in tight and hold, allowing myself to take a breath.

Dylan is wiggling against me, creating friction that pushes me to the edge. I pull out to the tip and take a breath. God, he feels good.

Realizing that I've been neglecting him, I pull all the way out and lean down to take his cock in my mouth. It's so hard that I can't help lick it up and down like a popsicle. The bead of cream at the end is like the cherry on top. Sliding my tongue inside, I'm able to steal a taste of him. After swirling my tongue across the head of his cock and down to suck his balls, I gently lick the rim of his hole. His cries of pleasure and writhing on the bed remind me of his need.

"I want you to come with me," I whisper as I lunge into him again. He nods and grabs his dick while I hold each of his calves out so he's fully stretched.

After just a few deep thrusts, I can't hold back anymore. "God, Dylan. Squeeze me. Take every drop." I arch my back and unload into him while he shoots onto his chest. His face is a vision of pure ecstasy. Beautiful, perfect ecstasy.

Chapter Twenty-Two

Dylan

By Sunday afternoon, we can hardly walk. Between switching positions and just general excursion, we're both exhausted and sore.

"I changed my flight to tomorrow morning." Spencer is laying half on top of me in my bed. "I'm not ready to leave."

"Then stay." I've been wanting to bring this up but didn't know how.

"What?" He lifts his head to meet my gaze. "What do you mean?"

"Stay here." I smile and lean in for a kiss. "Andre can oversee the repairs on the house and I know you can do your work from anywhere. So, just stay."

"Do you want me to?" I know he wouldn't have asked if he didn't want me to but I still need to hear him say it. I was looking for a relationship from the beginning but he's been resisting commitment.

"I do." Dylan tugs me so my face is beside his on the pillow. "I hate that you live so far away and I have to be here to keep an eye on everything. But I want you with me. Please stay."

I nod and take his lower lip between my teeth and pull off before going back in for more. "Yes." I pant as soon as I can get a word in. I'm not sure my body can take any more sex today but I'm sure as hell gonna give it the old college try.

~**~

"Do you really think you can get support for this?" Dylan is looking over my latest business plan. I spent the entire week in his bedroom working on this when I didn't have pressing matters for Styleopia to deal with.

I look over at him, lying across the foot of the bed with pages spread out in front of him. In just a pair of white boxer briefs on the white sheets. His darkly tanned body glows in the light of the setting sun and I can't help but smile and reach out to him. I'm not content unless I'm touching Dylan in some way. Based on how often he holds my hand or plays with the little hairs on the back of my neck, I know he feels the same.

"I do think I can." I run a finger across his rock hard abs. "And even if I can't, I'll fund it myself. This is important."

I had plans to work on a new app that connected distant relatives using public ancestry databases but that is now on the back burner.

"You're an amazing man, you know that?"

I shake my head. "It's not that hard and it can save lives. I don't know why no one has done it before." The new company I'm working on will provide group medical coverage to sex workers. After talking to Dylan about how much he has to pay for each of his employees to get quarterly STD tests and daily doses of PrEP, the HIV preventative meds that are required for all the boys in the stable, I realized how desperate the need is.

Most sex workers don't have access to medical care at all and can't afford preventative medicine so I've called in a few favors and made a large investment in an HMO. My mother would officially disown me if she found out about this project but I don't care.

I want to make sure Georgie and Scott and all the other people I've met recently can stay healthy while earning a living.

"Well, most people in your position wouldn't want to risk their name getting attached to something so uncouth."

"I've never been very couth." I slide my fingertips under the waistband of his boxers and tease his tip. "But I wouldn't trade this position for anything."

Read Patton's story in
More Than Friends #5: Hands On

More M/M Romance books by Aria Grace:

More Than Friends series

More Than Friends (#1)*

Drunk in Love (#2)*

Choosing Happy (#3)*

Just Stay (#4)*

Hands On (#5)*

Best Chance (#6)*

My Name is Luka (#7)*

Finally Found (#8)*

Looking For Home (#9)*

Choosing Us (#10)*

Mile High Romance series

When It's Right (#1)*

When I'm Weak (#2)*

When I'm Lost (#3)*

When You Were Mine (#4)*

When I Fall (#5)*

When Whiskey Stops Working (#6)

Promises Series
(M/M and M/F Contemporary)

Break Me Like a Promise (#1)

Trust Me Like a Promise (#2)

Keep Me Like a Promise (#3)

Real Answers Investigations series

Corner Office (#1)*

Soy Latte (#2)*

Cheers To That (#3)

Standalones

His Undoing (Gay For You)*

Winter Chill (First Time Gay)*

Escaping in Oz (College First Time)

*Also available as an audiobook

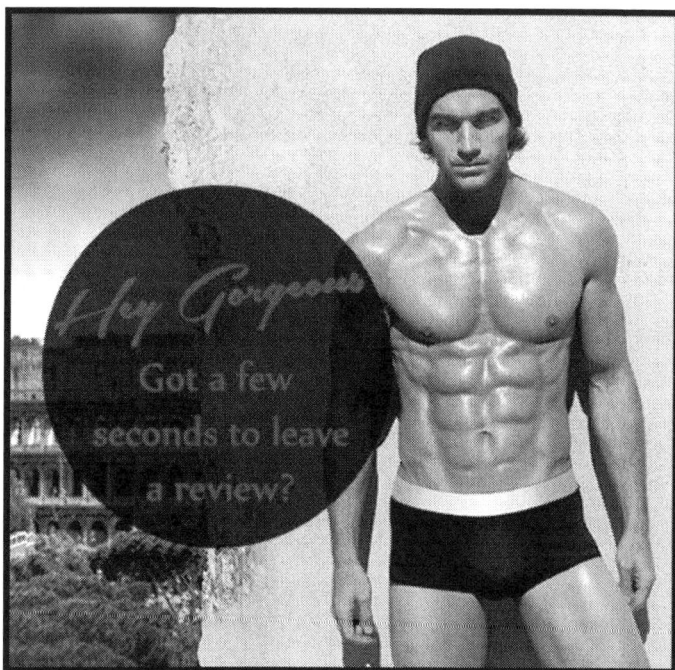

If you enjoyed this book, please consider leaving a review. Indie authors need all the support we can get. Thanks so much!

Learn more at www.AriaGraceBooks.com or become a kick ass fan and join my mailing list for updates and free book opportunities.

ariagracebooks@gmail.com

https://twitter.com/AriaGraceBooks

https://www.facebook.com/ariagracebooks

http://youtube.com/ariagracebooks

http://www.amazon.com/author/ariagrace

AN EXCERPT OF HANDS ON BY ARIA GRACE.

CHAPTER ONE

CALEB

When a shot glass is slammed on the table in front of me, sloshing tequila all over the Applied General Equilibrium Economics book I've been staring at for an hour, I know this is gonna be a shitty night. I've already had two tricks and it's not even eight thirty. I really need to study but I also need to make some cash.

I casually wipe the pages of my book with my sleeve and paste on my sexiest smile. I'm a professional and the sooner I graduate, the sooner I can stop peddling my ass and get a real job.

One look at the dirty Carhartts to my right and I know who the drink is from. Ron is becoming a regular but I'm not sure if that's a good thing. He can be cool when he's just drinking beer but tonight he's hit the tequila.

"Ron, hey." I lean back and push out the chair next to me with my foot. "Have a seat."

"Hey, baby." He drops heavily into the chair and looks at me from under his Seahawks hat. "You got a few minutes for me?"

"I always have time for you." I start stacking my books and glance at the clock above the register. "You ready now or do you want to finish your drink?"

"That's for you, baby." He scoots the shot closer as he lifts his own. "We'll drink together."

There's no way in hell I'm drinking anything he dropped in front of me. Especially not before going upstairs alone with him. I haven't known him for more than a few weeks so I need to stay alert.

"You're so sweet but I can't drink tonight." I pat the stack of books with my left hand as I scoot the glass to Ron. "I have to study tonight but I can wait while you finish both."

As the words come out, I know how stupid they are. He's obviously already had several. Two more shots are not going to make this night easier but it's too late now.

Ron just shakes his head as he pounds both shots in two breaths. His face pinches slightly but he's past the point of tasting it. I feel a slight shudder just witnessing it. I'd be puking by now if I tried that shit.

"You need to loosen up, kid." He stands and sways for a second, steading himself on the back of the chair. "You've always got your fucking nose buried in a book."

He's right. I try to look embarrassed by it but I'm not. I've worked hard to put myself through community college and I plan to transfer to Portland State in the fall. If I want to graduate within the next two years, I can't be getting drunk with frat boys every night.

I've spent the last two and a half years in this bar seven nights a week. When I'm not on Ray's payroll building drinks, I'm on my own payroll working tricks upstairs.

I'm not ashamed of where I'm at or how I got here. But I am eager to move past this point in my life. Just because my parents didn't want to watch their fairy son graduate from college or grow into a man, doesn't mean I'm not going to make it happen on my own. It does, however, mean I need to get through this fucking advanced equilibrium econ class and not get drunk tonight.

"I know." I stand and reach for his hand. He bypasses it and slides his arm around my waist instead, pulling me into his side forcefully. "But this is how I have fun."

As soon as we're alone in the office Ray allows me to use for tricks, Ron gets handsy. His beefy fingers close around the back of my neck and he guides me to the leather sofa. "I want you raw tonight, sweetheart."

I still under his hand. I don't do raw. Ever. I may have sex for money but I've never once had so much as a broken rubber. I'm clean and I intend to stay that way.

"You know I can't do that, Ron. I'd love to feel you inside me but Ray would cut me off if he found out." I turn up the charm and try to reason with him. "But I've got the magnum extra-large that I know you need. It'll still be tight on you but that'll just make it feel even better."

The buffoon buys my fake flattery and loosens his grip on my neck. "It better be fuckin huge because I've been rockin a goddamn log since I walked in."

He's not exceptionally well endowed but he's a man and he likes to be told his dick is big. Since he's paying me, I give him what his delicate ego needs. Reaching for his crotch, I smile. "Mmm, that's gonna feel so good."

"Fuck yeah it is." He thrusts into my hand. "Get it."

I guess we're done with the bedroom talk. With my hands under his shirt, I nudge him to the sofa. He falls into the middle of it and spreads his legs wide as he throws his head back, letting his arms rest on the cushions to either side of him.

I drop to my knees and unbutton his pants. If I don't move quick, he'll probably pass out. As much as I wouldn't mind if he did, I don't want to leave his two hundred pound ass up here all night while he sleeps it off so I need to get him in and out, literally, as soon as possible.

Once his dick is released from his jeans, his hand is back around my neck. Ron only allows me a few seconds to pull the condom from my pocket and get it in place before he's bucking into my mouth. I try to just relax and take it but his grip is tight, causing my whole body to tense.

I know fighting it isn't going to help but I can't stop myself from trying to pull off. Of course, he isn't having any of that. Ron gets off on the panicked look in my eyes and smiles as I twist my shoulders, trying to get air into my burning lungs.

"That's it, baby. Take it good." His other hand rakes across the top of my head until the heel of his palm is at my forehead. He curls his fingers, tugging my fine hair into the sweaty crevices of his hand. Normally, I like to have my hair pulled a little bit but between the pain on my neck and the extended periods between each breath, I go into full-on panic mode.

My jaw instinctively clenches and I bite the base of Ron's cock. Hard. His fist rips my head away from him and he swings my whole body to the ground. "What the fuck, Caleb. You think that shit is funny?"

He grabs the front of my shirt and lifts me straight up then tosses me onto the couch.

"I'm sorry, babe. I didn't mean to." I turn my head into my shoulder to rub my stinging eyes. "I couldn't breathe for a minute there and I think my survival instincts kicked in."

He's lucky I didn't bite that shit off.

I smile and pretend my breathlessness is lust-induced as I reach for him. "Let me make it up to you."

He looks around the room for a second like he's not sure how to respond. Finally, he exhales loudly then seems to get back into it. When his softening dick starts to fill up, I know we're back in business. I sit up and run my fingers down his arm and across his belly. "Just lay back and I'll do all the work."

"Uh uh." He grabs the waistband of my jeans and pulls me up. "Take these off and bend over the side."

Trying to keep my smile sexy instead of disgusted, I unzip my skinny jeans and push them down to my ankles. I don't usually wear underwear so once I step out and yank my shirt off, I'm fully bare to Ron.

"That's right, baby." He runs a finger over my nipple then down to the tip of my dick. "You're gonna like this."

I'm semi hard. Not enough to prove actual interest in him but enough to prove I'm a virile man of twenty-three and can keep it up for as long as I need to. "How do you want me?"

Without actual words, he grunts and positions me on all fours across the sofa. My head is hanging over the armrest, just waiting for his intrusion.

"Lube's on the table, baby." I left it out earlier and hope he'll be generous. I haven't been fucked in a few days and I know I'm tighter than I like to be with guys like Ron. Guys that like it rough. Most guys come in for a quick blow job and are on their way but Ron is gonna make me earn my hundred bucks tonight.

"The rubber has enough." He pokes a few fingers inside me for about five seconds before they are replaced by his dry dick. "You want me to wear this shit, you must like the way they feel."

I bite my lip and squeeze my eyes shut as he pounds into me. Dry. This will be the last time that fucker touches me. I'll play nice tonight but I'll let Tony know to keep him away from me. Tony is the big ass bar manager on the floor most nights I'm here and is like the brother I've never had.

Once Ron is fully seated inside me, his hands wrap around my waist and dig into my skin. I'm gonna have bruises on both sides but at least that pain is a small distraction from the fire shooting through me as my skin tears with each thrust.

I feel like he's been riding me for an hour but it's probably only been a few minutes before he picks up his pace. Since there is less friction, I have to assume my blood is acting as lube and I'm thankful when he finally shoots his load. I just pray that condom didn't break with the abuse it's endured because I don't trust this mother fucker as far as I could throw him.

"You always feel so good, baby." Ron is gentle now as he pulls out and tosses the messy condom on the floor. "I could do this every day."

Over my dead body.

"Um hmm…" I carefully slide out from under him and grab my jeans. "That was amazing."

He wants to cuddle but I manage to get dressed. "Can I at least buy you a drink now?"

"I wish I could." I hand him his pants and pick up our trash. Wrapping everything in a few tissues, I drop it in waste basket under the table. "Maybe next time."

Ron stands and reaches for his wallet. "Here's a little extra for taking it like a champ."

He gives me a wet kiss as he slips a few bills in my hand. I don't bother to look at them as I tuck the cash into my back pocket. Turning toward the cabinet where I keep a container of Lysol wipes, I say over my shoulder, "Thanks, Ron. I've got to clean up in here before I head down."

"See you in a few days, baby."

I don't look back until I hear his heavy steps moving down the staircase.

Chapter Two

Patton

I'm just pulling a microwave lasagna out of the freezer when my phone rings. It's Finn. I debate whether or not to answer but I know he'll keep calling until I do. On the third ring, I pick it up.

"Hello." As much as I try to sound pleasant, I know my voice is just annoyed.

"Oh, Patton, hey. I'm glad I caught you." He doesn't sound glad. He sounds disappointed that he can't just leave a message.

"Uh, Finn? Is that you?" He doesn't need to know that I'd never forget his voice. That it haunts my dreams and still stars in all my fantasies. "What's up?"

"I need a favor." Of course he does. Why else would he call me? When he dumped me for the drummer in our band—my band—he made it very clear I wasn't what he wanted anymore.

"And what's that?" I hate myself for even asking. I shouldn't be considering helping this asshole in any way. Not after the way he broke my heart. I thought the distance between us was because he was working longer hours, maybe saving up for a ring or something, but I was naïve. He was working on Jack.

If I learned nothing else from my time with Finn, at least I'll never give my heart so fully and freely to someone that I don't completely know and trust.

"I'm applying for a job at the court house and I need you to be a reference. They want people that have known me for more than two years. Just tell them how responsible I am and that you'd totally hire me." He laughs. "You know, lie."

I force a laugh. "Yeah, that would be a lie."

"So you'll do it?"

Seriously? I groan but I can't refuse. He needs a good job and maybe seeing defendants in courtrooms day in and day out will help set him on a better path in life. "I guess."

"Thanks, man." He's quiet for a second then remembers to ask about me. "So how are things out in Portland? Rain enough for you?"

Just because it doesn't rain that much in Colorado Springs doesn't make it a better conversation starter. But, at least he's trying. "Things are great. I'm working at a nice spa and have met a few people. I love it here."

See, I can lie with the best of them. Truth is, I haven't really met anyone except the single mom that lives downstairs and the girls at work. Everyone's been nice enough but there isn't anyone that I'd actually call a friend.

"Good to hear it." He sounds distracted and there's rustling around on the line. "Okay, I'll let you go. Thanks, man."

"Yeah. Bye."

I shouldn't have a pit in my stomach just from talking to him. I want to be over Finn. I need to be over Finn. But despite the months that have passed and the knowledge that he's clearly moved on without a backward glance, I still want to cry.

No more of this whiney shit, Patton!

I put the Lean Cuisine back in the freezer and head to my room. I'm going out tonight. There's a bar Heather told me about that I've been wanting to check out. No reason why tonight shouldn't be the night.

After a quick shower and a power bar, I head over to Ray's. Heather, the woman that lives below me with her year old daughter, said it's a quiet spot to shoot some pool or just have a drink. That's exactly what I need.

When I walk in, I'm surprised how busy it is for seven PM on a Wednesday. Pop music is playing in the background and several groups of people are seated at tables around the place. There are some open high tops but I don't want to sit alone.

A stool in the middle of the bar seems innocuous enough so I slip onto it and take a look around. This doesn't look like most of the gay bars I've been to but they're definitely gay-friendly, if the small rainbow flag above the register is any indicator. It's actually the only indicator.

Most of the patrons are guys but that's true in most bars. Regardless, I'm not here to pick up anyone. That's not my style. I'm just here for a drink and to feel like a regular guy again. I've missed not having the guys from the band to have a drink with on weekends or after gigs.

By the time I turn back around, the bartender is standing in front of me. "Can I get you something?"

"Tanqueray and Tonic, please."

He smiles and nods. "You got it."

With what I hope isn't taken as anything more than polite curiosity, I watch the kid reach for the bottle from the top shelf. His shirt pulls up slightly, revealing the creamy white skin of his slender hips, peeking out from his dark, tight jeans. The boy looks young—younger than he must be if he's a pouring drinks, but hot.

I'm still staring when he turns around and pours the liquor into a highball. I slowly let my gaze crawl up his chest to his face. He's not looking at me so I study his delicate features and streaked blond hair. It's not too short but you can tell he likes to look good and puts effort into it.

The time he takes is well spent. He's hot as hell. When I glance at him, his crystal blue eyes are trained on me. I want to look away but I can't. He winks then hands me the glass. "Here ya go. That'll be eight bucks."

I pull out a ten and hand it to the kid. When he tries to give me my change, I just shake my head and take a sip. The citrusy drink is smooth and only briefly reminds me of Finn.

As I nurse my drink, I can't help but watch the sexy bartender. He has an easy smile and an infectious laugh. He's clearly liked by all his customers and enjoys chatting them up. Every now and then I catch his eye and he smiles, but then he glances down to my glass to see if I'm ready for a refill. When I finally finish my drink, he's in front of me before the glass meets the wood.

"Ready for another?" He's wiping out the inside of a glass as he waits for my answer.

"Um, yeah." I slide the empty glass to him. "Just one more. I don't usually drink much on work nights."

He nods turns to grab the bottle of Tanqueray. "That's usually a good policy."

He moves gracefully as he prepares my drink. Since I've spent the past thirty minutes watching the poor guy, I've noticed he rolls his shoulders and stretches his neck often.

Before he slides my drink to me, I lay down another ten.

He pulls two singles from the register and tries to hand them to me but I just shake my head. "Keep it."

"Thanks." He drops them into a jar on the back wall and comes back to me. "I haven't seen you in before. Just visiting?"

I take a drink before responding. "New to town. I've only been in the area for a few months."

"Cool." His hand moves to his left shoulder and he rubs circles while nodding slowly. "Where are you from?"

"Colorado." I watch his hand move from his shoulder to his neck. "You got a kink?"

"Oh, yeah." He drops his hand self-consciously. "Occupational hazard."

I look left and right, confused by the comment. "I didn't realize bartending was so dangerous."

He gives me another wink. "It can be."

A guy leans in on my right and places his elbow on the bar beside me, brushing against my back. I bristle at the unexpected contact and lean away.

"Caleb, can you send a couple Cokes to the back when you get a chance?" The man is large with full tattoo sleeves on both arms. He looks like a body builder so I don't look too closely. If he's straight, he probably won't appreciate me checking him out.

"You got it, Steve," Caleb responds.

Caleb. I like it. He looks like a Caleb.

"Thanks, gorgeous." The man drops a twenty on the counter and walks away.

I let out a low whistle. "Damn, Cokes are expensive in here."

He laughs and rings up the drinks then drops the 300% tip in the jar. "He's a good friend."

"I see." If that guy is calling him gorgeous and leaving tips like that, I'm sure he's more than just a friend.

Caleb gives me smirk that tells me he knows what I'm thinking. I hope my snide comment didn't sound as petty as it could have.

When Caleb walks away to place the Cokes on a tray, I turn in my stool and look around again. It's gotten a little busier but I can still see to the billiard tables in the back. The guy, Steve, is playing with a young blond that looks even younger than Caleb. This kid is barely legal. But by the way they watch each other and stop to kiss between almost every shot, it's clear Steve isn't interested in Caleb.

When I spin back around, Caleb is taking a picture of two girls holding up pink drinks at the far end of the bar. When he hands the phone back to them, he notices me watching him. His hand moves to his neck and rubs it while he smiles broadly at me. "Do you need anything else?"

My glass is still half full so I can't use that as an excuse. Besides, I have to work tomorrow and I don't want to feel like shit all day. "No, thanks. But I can probably help with your neck." I take a final drink then stand. "I just started working as a massage therapist at Hydrate Day Spa. Come by and I'll comp a massage."

Caleb takes the card I hand him and looks at it for a minute before understanding dawns. "Oh, my neck." He smiles shyly. "Thanks, I might do that."

Read more of Patton and Caleb's story in

More Than Friends #5: Hands On

Made in the USA
Middletown, DE
07 August 2024